DATING
in
the **DARK**

Also By
Alexandria Bishop

Marlowe Series
Finding Flynn
Falling for Hudson
Freeing Jude
Fighting for Jax

Rescuing Maria

Dating Trilogy
Dating in the Dark
Sinking in the Shadows
Loving in the Light

DATING *in the* DARK

ALEXANDRIA BISHOP

ISBN-13: 978-1981456703
ISBN-10: 1981456708

Cover Design by Mischievous Designs

Edited by Editing by C. Marie
Proofread by Ellie McLove

First Edition:
10 9 8 7 6 5 4 3 2

To my readers,
Thank you for sticking with me
Through everything!
I hope you enjoy
Tinley & Marek's story!

ONE

*N*ine-fifteen.

It's been approximately thirty seconds since the last time Tinley glanced at the clock in the bottom corner of her monitor. Her shift started an hour and fifteen minutes ago, and yet her phone remains silent. The delicious sweet nectar of coffee she was drinking is long gone, and her caffeine high is quickly fading due to boredom. Her purse is hiding a delicious strawberries and cream cupcake that she was using as something to look forward to later in the day, but desperate times call for desperate measures, and the fluffy melt-in-your-mouth buttercream is calling her name.

"Domestic," whispers the voice in her headset, alerting her to a call coming in from one of their United States customers.

"Thank you for calling Wanderlust International, my name is Tinley, can I cure your lust for adventure with a Caribbean cruise today?" She tries not to choke on her words as they tumble out of her overly fake, plastered-on smile because, as her boss likes to drill into her head every single day she's at this damn job, the customer can hear a smile in your voice. As it turns out, Tinley would rather vomit than spend one more minute caring what these customers think.

"Am I on a recorded line right now?" Tinley pulls the headset away from her ear and turns the volume way down. There are some conversations where she has to struggle to hear a single word, but ones like this, for example, are projected just fine. It's annoying, but just part of the job. "I'm not sure how I feel about that, and I don't think I ever gave y'all permission to record me."

Every freaking time. She doesn't know what it is, but it's like they completely ignore everything until they're talking to a real person. This lady must be one of those zero pressers who keeps hitting it no matter what the recording says. News flash lady, it doesn't always work that way.

Tinley quickly mutes her phone, chugs down some water, fake screams, unmutes her phone, and plasters on her fake smile again. Using a saccharine yet professional voice, she says, "Ma'am, you are on a recorded line. We record all of our phone calls for quality assurance and training."

Before the woman even starts talking again, Tinley can sense the anger already starting to build. "But you didn't tell me that. Aren't you required by law to tell me you're recording me? I have yet to hear those words come out of your mouth."

"I apologize for any confusion ma'am. Before you were connected to me, the line did let you know you were being recorded, and like I said, we record all calls for quality assurance and training."

The audible breathing on the other end of the call becomes heavier and heavier. It's T-minus five minutes until explosion time. Hell, if Tinley's lucky, this call will be ending in less time, and she can go for a "smoke break," even though she doesn't smoke. Around here, it seems to be the only acceptable excuse for abandoning your station for five minutes; God forbid she has to pee or—heaven help us—change a tampon. Nope, the dudes running this place don't want to hear about the woes of being a woman, and it has become common practice for everything to be described as a smoke break.

Whatever.

"I don't like the tone you're taking with me. I am the customer, and if I didn't exist, you wouldn't have a job right now. You think about that one, missy. Isn't the first thing they teach you people that I am always right?"

Another holier-than-thou customer who seems to think she knows all—just what Tinley was hoping for to end her perfect suckfest of a week. With a quick glance at the clock, she inwardly groans. She's killed exactly three more minutes of her day; only seven more hours until she's free from this place for an entire forty-eight hours, but who's counting?

"I'm really sorry if I upset you. I would be glad to help you out today in any way I can." Her back stiffens when someone starts hooting and hollering in the corner, no doubt the current largest sale for the day. It probably went to that douchebag, Marek Outlaw. While he's not technically her boss, he's still a supervisor on the floor. He's never ever on the phones, but if he pops on for five minutes? He always lands the biggest deals. What kind of a last name is Outlaw anyway? It has to be fake.

"It's a little too late for apologies. I think you need to transfer me to a manager and find a new job. You're obviously no good at this one."

"One moment please, I'll transfer you right over. Before I do, is there anything else I can help you with?"

"No, you can't. I would like to talk to someone with intelligence, although I'm not holding my breath on that since someone obviously had to train you."

Six hours and forty-two minutes. Only six hours and forty-two minutes to go.

"I hope you enjoy the rest of your day ma'am. Transferring now." She hits transfer and blows out everything she was holding back. "And fuck you very much, you cow."

Damn, that didn't even help a little bit in helping her feel better. She remembers back in the good old days when a fervent one-finger salute to her computer and headset was all it took to cheer her up. Now? Not even the nightly after-work cocktails are helping. Something needs to change, that's for damn sure.

She puts her phone on *unavailable* so another call can't come through then turns to her neighbor. It just so happens to be her best friend and roommate, Dakota—who, by the way, got the better end of the stick with this job because she only answers emails and the occasional chat. Meanwhile, Tinley deals with all the jerks over the phone.

"Shoot me now. Please just take me into the back room, whack me over the head, and be done with it. I'm ready to meet my maker and own up to the shit I've done in this life for the kind of karma being thrown my way. I would much rather be dead than deal with another phone call like that."

Dakota continues typing her bullshit response to some crazy she's got in a chat and says, "Okay drama queen. I'm going to keep saying it until it makes it through that thick skull of yours: You. Need. To. Get. Laid. Plain and simple."

"Don't worry, Tinley, I can fix that for you."

She doesn't even look up to see who's speaking; she knows it's Marek. She rolls her eyes and instead, the trusty one-finger salute goes up in the air. His arrogance really bugs the shit out of her, and the problem is he knows how badly he gets under her skin. She ignores him completely and continues talking to Dakota. "Do you ever think about anything else besides sex? It's not the cure-all for every single problem out there, you know."

"Says the woman who never gets any." Dakota points to herself and looks up from her computer screen to look Tinley in the eyes. "Am I ever half as stressed as you? I know you say you don't give a shit about this job, but you always seem awfully worked up over something you supposedly care so little about."

"If you had to deal with—"

Dakota raises her hand as she turns her monitor toward Tinley, and the crude language spewed all over her computer screen is absolutely disgusting. Her eyes zero in on one line from the chat. "Is it really necessary for you to know *that* happened on the cruise? C'mon, doesn't this person have any self-respect?"

She pops her gum and sends a final response before ending the chat and locking her computer. "Tinley, the keyboard warriors aren't afraid to say anything and everything as long as the words are being typed and not actually spoken. You'd be surprised at the crap people say to me every day, but unlike you, I don't let it affect me. This is a job, nothing more."

"And that is why you'll never be up for a promotion. You're not a team player, Dakota."

Tinley is annoyed that Marek is still standing there. If he weren't so smug and arrogant, she would actually be attracted to him. His low husky voice is enough to make any woman's panties wet, including hers. She rolls her eyes and wills her phone to start ringing so she can avoid whatever confrontation is about to happen. Then she remembers she put it on *unavailable* and resigns herself to another annoying co-worker encounter.

"You say that like it's a bad thing." Her best friend laughs and walks away, leaving Tinley all alone with the gorgeous dickbag. Why are the attractive ones always the biggest jerks?

Closing her eyes, she takes a deep breath and slowly turns around to find him standing directly behind her. "Is there something I can help you with Marek?" She inwardly cringes as her voice cracks. *Way to go Tinley, real smooth.*

"I just got off the phone with one of your customers, and she wasn't too happy with the interaction she had with you. Fortunately, I was able to save the sale, no thanks to you."

Ugh. The last thing she is in the mood for is a lecture from Marek "The Asshole" Outlaw, and why the hell did Dakota just leave her all alone with this jerk? She's going to have to have a chat with her about the rules of best friend loyalty because this right here definitely breaks them. "Sorry, it's time for my smoke break. Can we talk about this later?"

Marek gives her a double take then shakes his head. He's a got a smug grin on his face, and she can't decide if she would rather slap it off or sit on it. The former would probably be a lot more satisfying. Marek is probably one of those guys who seems like he would be good in bed but is actually all about himself and makes for a really lousy experience. "You don't even smoke, and it's not your break time."

"Are you sure about that? Are you one hundred percent sure that I don't smoke? Because Jonah over there just came in from a smoke break and I know he takes more than the allotted two fifteen-minute breaks a day. So, unless you're going to tell every person in here who smokes that they're only allowed to do that on their given breaks, I don't think you can play favorites and tell me I can't spend five minutes away from my desk getting a cup of coffee, shoving a tampon in, or doing any other thing I feel the need to do to clear my head of the assholes on the phone."

Mic drop.

Tinley's hands are shaking as she walks away from Marek and heads toward the front doors. She can't believe she said any of those things to him. She's never stood up to him like that before, and she kind of liked it. As the doors slide open and she's hit with a major heat wave, all she can do is smile. Not able to walk out the doors without one last look, she turns around slightly and slams right into Jonah on his way out for his umpteenth smoke break of the day. To make matters worse, she was trying to be cute and spin on one foot, and all that did was cause her to lose her balance. Her legs fly out from underneath her, and her butt slams down on the track of the sliding doors.

Someone starts a slow clap, and laughter can be heard throughout the office. Unmistakably, Marek's timber thunders over everyone else's. Tinley has never been particularly graceful, but this one moment would have been the perfect time for her to pull it off. Instead, her grace is lying down in the gutter, along with her dignity. Her body screams out in pain as she slowly pushes herself up—not a single person came running to offer their help. A bunch of selfish jerks, all of them. Her foot slides as she steadies herself on her feet and she almost face-plants into the cement, but fortunately she catches herself before that can happen. The doors finally shut behind her as she walks away on her hunt for her so-called best friend.

There's no way this day could get any worse, right?

TWO

*W*orst day ever.

The day started out slow, hit an all-time high with her confrontation with Marek, and then quickly crashed and burned with her wipe out, and it didn't get much better for Tinley after that. No matter what happened, it seemed like she couldn't do anything right, and the customers—*ugh*. Today was full of customers from hell. That's the only explanation for why every single one of them got worse as each additional call came in. Not a single person she talked to purchased a vacation package, and in fact, they all seemed to think they'd won free vacation packages and were redeeming them. She hopes whoever the scammers were that made up that little stunt get herpes and syphilis—really gross and painful and makes their dicks fall off.

Of course, it's Friday, so every second of the day felt like it took hours to go by. Combine the long day with shitty customers, and it's left Tinley pretty much wiped out, which is why she is currently on her second glass of wine as she's preparing tonight's dinner. Tinley, Dakota, and Tinley's sister, Tara, have a standing dinner date the second Friday of every month, and Tinley is always in charge of the food. She's not complaining about it because the other two don't know their way around a microwave, let alone the entire kitchen. Having either one of them cook is just a recipe for disaster. That and a visit to the takeout menu drawer in their kitchen.

She is grateful that she's had the past hour to herself in the apartment. After spending all day on a headset talking to people, her ears are always buzzing, and need some peace and quiet. The one good thing about Tinley and Dakota working in different departments is that they have different work schedules. Tinley goes in an hour earlier, so she's off first. Unfortunately, she knows her silence is about to disappear as she takes another quick glance at the clock. Dakota and Tara will be here any minute now.

As if on cue, the familiar sound of her best friend's key turning in the deadbolt sounds with a click. Laughter echoes throughout the dwelling as Tinley puts the last dish she used to prepare the meal into the dishwasher. The casserole she made has been cooling on the counter for a good fifteen minutes now, and the coffee aroma from the mocha cupcakes that are currently baking in the oven has started permeating the air. If any of the cupcakes make it past the weekend, she's hoping the extra caffeine kick will help her get through what is sure to be a hellish Monday. Judging by her current mood, she won't be holding her breath on that one.

As soon as they walk into the room, Dakota zeroes in on the open bottle of wine. Whenever Tinley ventures out and buys a new wine, Dakota always has to inspect it like she's a fancy connoisseur. In reality, everyone knows she has no idea what she's doing, but as always, she picks up the bottle of Pinot Grigio and takes a small whiff. She swirls the contents of the bottle and takes a small taste straight from the container. With an annoyingly long glance at the label, she shrugs and pours herself a glass. "You have to tell Tara about the conversation you had with Marek this morning." Then she walks out of the room toward her bedroom, no doubt to grab her laptop like she does every night after work.

Tinley knows she should be happy Dakota isn't once again ragging on her about how much she needs to get laid, but the excitement over her little showdown with Marek this morning won't last long. As much as it felt good at the time, she has felt like nothing but crap for the rest of the day since, which is why after finishing preparing dinner tonight, Tinley decided it would be a good idea to bake another batch of cupcakes, even though they still haven't finished off the last ones she made. No doubt her sister will have her arms full of cupcakes when she leaves tonight. Her whole argument that she's "eating for two," can only go so far. In reality, Tinley knows she gets mad cravings for sweets when she's pregnant.

Tara tilts her head to the side then looks from Dakota to Tinley and back again. She rubs her belly and crashes back into their very plush recliner. "Marek—is he the panty-melting fuckboy that always seems to annoy you?"

No words—Tinley has absolutely no words for what just came out of her sister's mouth. Who even talks like that? Tinley giggles and feels nothing but embarrassment for her. Still, she tops off her own glass of wine and grabs a sparkling water out of the fridge for Tara before joining her in the living room. "Please never say any of those words ever again. I'm going to assume that what you're trying to say is he is fucking gorgeous, if so, then yes he is one in the same. The arrogant asshole that we work with. It's really unreasonable for how good looking he is."

And it's true. Tinley knows Marek is way completely outside of her league, but it doesn't stop her from lusting after him no matter how much she hates herself for doing it. He's the kind of attractive where he knows he is and doesn't hide that knowledge one bit. The supervisors all get to choose who is on their team, and of course, Marek has built his own fraternity in his corner of the call center. Or at least that's what Dakota and her like to refer to them as. All of the guys on his team are all just as arrogant as Marek is and they all treat him like he's a god or something. It's actually kind of sickening.

Dakota plops down on the couch next to her and

immediately starts tapping away on her laptop, completely oblivious to the conversation going on around her...or maybe she just doesn't care. It's weird because she spends all day typing on a computer and then comes home and spends all night doing the same thing. This has been going on for months now, Tinley has bugged her on multiple occasions to spill about what she's doing, but she's been pretty tight-lipped so far.

Tara shrugs and takes a heavy drink from her bottle of water and adds, "What can I say? I'm hip. I know what the cool kids are saying these days. I'm in the know."

"Don't make me laugh."

Tara ignores Tinley's comment and turns her focus to her sister's roommate. "Dakota, please tell your roommate I'm superfly."

That grabs her attention, and she finally looks up from her computer, but just barely. She takes another swig from her wine glass before placing it back on the coffee table and saying, "Tinley, your sister has no idea what she's talking about. Don't ever listen to her."

She sits forward on the edge of her seat, and her mouth drops open. "Hey, you're supposed to be on my side here."

"Dude, I'm on nobody's side." Dakota doesn't even look up from her screen as she continues working away on whatever she's writing. "But if you keep talking like that, you're just going to make a fool of yourself."

"Neither of you know what you're talking about. Livi thinks I'm awesome."

Tinley can't hold in her laughter any longer after that statement. "That's because she's seven and your daughter. Of course, she thinks you're awesome—you're the only person she knows."

"I don't even know why I keep coming to these things. I don't have to put up with this abuse. I can get my sugar fix elsewhere, you know."

"Oh my gosh, Tara, you sound exactly like Mom right now. And you know nobody makes their cupcakes as good as I can. I happen to recall you telling me I should open my own bakery."

"No, I don't. You take that back right now." She sneers at Tinley and then quickly changes the subject and her focus. "Dakota, what are you working on over there?"

Before her roommate can answer, Tinley pipes up. "Don't even try to get her to tell you. It's some sort of top-secret project she's been working on. She refuses to tell me, and this has been going on for months now. At this point, it's more annoying than anything else."

She quickly closes her laptop and puts it on the coffee table in front of her. "Anyone else starving? Let's eat." Then she's up from the couch and heading off to the kitchen for the casserole, which is most likely cold by now.

Tara glances behind her to see if Dakota is watching and then leans forward, reaching for the laptop. Tinley shakes her head and says, "Don't even bother. She has it password protected." Reaching a hand down to help her up, she says, "C'mon preggo, let's go get some food in that belly."

Speaking of the cupcakes, the timer starts going off as they both walk toward the kitchen. The entire room is filled with the delicious chocolatey coffee scent, and Tinley can't help but breathe them in as she pulls them out of the oven to cool.

Dakota has a second bottle of wine open and is drinking from her recently refilled glass as she studies the casserole dish on the counter. "Someone gave zero fucks when they cut the vegetables for tonight's dinner."

Tinley takes a sip of her glass of wine before glancing down into the food and shrugging. If this were a competition based solely on presentation, she would be asked to never return. She lets out a small giggle. Okay, so she might be buzzing just a little bit. "I always say Anne Burrell would have a field day with my knife cuts if we ever shared the same kitchen."

"Am I supposed to know what that means?"

Face meet palm. There's no way her roommate doesn't know who she's talking about. Tinley spends her free time watching TV, and when Netflix isn't on, the Food Network is. "Hello, Anne Burrell, as in the celebrity chef from the Food Network. She co-hosts the show *Worst Cooks in America*, and she always cracks down on people for their knife cuts. I might make good food, but I can't consistently cut anything to save my life."

A moan comes from behind them, and both girls turn around to find Tara already working her way through the dinner. She's got a giant spoon in her hand and is leaning over the counter, scooping out bites. "I don't care what it looks like as long as it tastes good, and this definitely tastes fanfuckingtastic."

All three of them crack up laughing as they take turns devouring the semi-warm casserole, and Tara's right: it is pretty damn good. Then again, anything involving potatoes, cheese, and bacon usually is. After they finish polishing off dinner, Tinley starts putting the dishes in the sink to clean everything up. If there's one thing she hates more than anything, it's a dirty kitchen. She just can't focus while there's a mess nearby.

Dakota takes the dirty forks out of her hands and shoos her away. Tinley sits on one of the bar stools and takes a small sip of her wine while looking from her sister to her roommate over the top of her glass. These two are definitely up to something, that's for sure. Dakota never volunteers to clean up the kitchen and Tara is avoiding eye contact altogether. "Okay, what's going on here? What are you two hiding from me?"

Tara sighs and leans against the counter. She polishes off her bottle of water and rubs her belly. She glances over at Dakota and then back at her sister. "Promise you won't be mad?"

THREE

*U*nease builds in the pit of Tinley's stomach. This doesn't sound good at all. "Mad about what?"

"You have plans tomorrow night."

"Um, no I don't." She thinks for a minute...is she supposed to be babysitting for her sister? She doesn't remember agreeing to that, but it's possible she just forgot, or...*oh no!* She's not trying to set her up with a guy from Clark's work again, is she? Every time her sister tries to set her up with one of her husband's co-workers, it always ends in disaster. Tinley treads lightly as she asks, "What are you talking about?"

Tara nibbles on the bottom of her lip and her eyes travel around the room. She avoids eye contact with Tinley at all costs and then turns her focus to Dakota. "You tell her, Dakota—she'll take it better from you."

"No way." She shakes her head and waves her hands in the air. "This whole thing was your idea. I just found out about it and told you. You're the one who actually signed her up."

The back and forth banter between her sister and roommate does nothing but make her head spin. The two of them have an intense stare down making Tinley want to scream for someone to say something. They can't build up all of this anxiety in her and not at least tell her what's going on.

"Fine, be a big baby about it." Tara turns back toward Tinley and turns on her mom voice. "We signed you up for a blind date. Well sort of. It's kind of hard to explain what it is exactly."

And all that explanation does is confuse Tinley even more. How could they have signed her up for something and not know how to explain it to her? That doesn't make any sense at all. She releases a huff in frustration and asks, "Okay, what does that mean?"

Dakota groans in frustration and walks back into the living room. When she comes back, she has her laptop in hand. "Oh, for fuck's sake, it's speed dating in the dark—super short dates, and you don't get to see the dude you're on a date with, kind of like the blind auditions on *The Voice*. The whole point is to get to know someone without any kind of biases involved."

Tinley chokes on the last bit of wine that she was in the process of draining from her glass. They can't be serious about this. Can they? Speed dating in the dark?

That sounds completely made up. "Wait, you're kidding me, right? Are you just making all of this up? Not that it's a very good story. Speed dating in the dark? There's no way that would ever actually be a thing."

Tinley's mouth falls open as Dakota places her laptop on the bar in front of her. Sure enough, there's a flyer inviting her to speed date in the dark at a local restaurant, and yep, the event is tomorrow night. Why the hell would they sign her up for something so ridiculous? Her empty wine glass comes into focus out of the corner of her eye. She's going to need another drink and a strong one at that. Wine just isn't going to cut it at this point.

She grabs the bottle of tequila out of the freezer and a shot glass out of the cupboard. She quickly slams back one shot, and then a second. The familiar burn is welcomed as it slides down her throat and into her belly; anything to get her mind off of the information she was just given. Joining in on the fun, Dakota takes a couple of shots as well.

Tara shakes her head and rubs her belly while watching the two of them get completely hammered. "As much fun as it is watching you two polish off a bottle of tequila, this preggo has to get going. If I don't get home and take off this bra and these pants soon, I might just have to strip down naked right here. My boobs and belly are currently screaming for freedom. You two have a fun night—just don't get too drunk."

Tinley cringes at that picture. Her sister is wearing a pair of leggings and a tunic. How that could possibly feel restricting makes zero sense to her. Pregnancy sounds like the last thing she'd ever want to do. She couldn't even picture herself with a giant belly with a baby inside. Besides, in order to make a baby, you have to have sex and Tinley doesn't even want to think about how long it's been since the last time that happened. Nope, pregnancy is not something that is in her near future, if ever.

"Gross. Dakota, please remind me to never get pregnant, ever."

Dakota leans over and offers up her hand for a high-five. "You and me both sister. We'll make a pact on that right now. No babies for these bitches. Ever."

Tara laughs and points at both of them. "You say that now, but then next thing you know, you'll both be knocked up, just like me." She walks over to Tinley and offers her a hug. "Please don't be mad at us, okay? We're just trying to help you out."

"I'm too drunk right now to be mad. Ask me again in the morning, and I might be able to give you a better answer. I'm almost thirty, Tara, and this is my life. I'm not a project or something for you to fix."

She knows they both mean well, but this was definitely not the way to help her. Speed dating? Seriously? Who even does that? She always thought it was some crazy thing they slipped into thirty-minute sitcoms to mix things up, you know, when things start getting stale and they need a little something extra to add to the storyline and make people laugh so they can forget about their miserable existence—and yes, Tinley would happen to be one of those people.

Dakota walks over to the coffee table and grabs her laptop, hugging it to her chest. *Odd.* "I'm heading to bed now, do you need anything from me?"

She eyes the bottle of tequila still sitting on the counter and contemplates another shot. The combination of the wine and liquor sloshing in her stomach makes her slightly nauseous. It probably wasn't a good idea mixing. She quickly puts the cap back on and stashes the bottle in the back of the freezer buried underneath a bag of frozen veggies. Logically she knows that won't keep her from drinking it, but maybe it'll be a slight deterrent.

"Nope, I'm good. I think I'll do the same."

They both walk down the hallway to their separate bedrooms, and when Tinley closes the door behind her, her own laptop comes into focus. She needs to do an internet search on this whole dating-in-the-dark thing. It can't be that common, can it? Fortunately, the first link that pops up is exactly what she's looking for. What she's surprised to find is that they run these events in almost every major city. Who would have thought?

Speed dating...in the dark...with a stranger. What were those two thinking? Tinley continues looking over the site, which is filled with what has to be a bunch of stock photos because nobody in their right mind looks that happy going to speed dating. *Ugh.* Just thinking about it makes her queasy. Or maybe that's the tequila again?

Fifteen minutes—that's all you get to find the man of

your dreams. A small chuckle escapes from her mouth. Nobody in their right mind can actually believe they'll find their true love in fifteen minutes, and if anyone does feel that way, she just feels sorry for them. Finding your soul mate at speed dating—oh yeah, that'll go over about as well as a nun in a strip club. And not the sexy kind either. The legit full-gown virginal nun. She giggles just picturing that in her head. What reason would a nun have to step foot into a strip club? Her giggle fit continues on for a few seconds. Maybe she's still a little buzzed after all?

She slams her laptop shut and releases a heavy sigh. Throwing herself back onto her bed, she contemplates the situation. Sure, her thirtieth birthday is coming up, and she isn't in a serious relationship, but Dakota isn't either. She's a grown-ass woman and doesn't need her best friend and sister telling her how to live her life. It's not like their lives are perfect either.

That's it, in the morning she'll just tell them both that she won't be going. The whole thing is silly anyway. How mad can they be about it? It's just a stupid speed dating thing, it's not like they could really be all that serious about it. And it's not like they can force her to go anyway. Right?

FOUR

*T*here's a knock on Tinley's bedroom door, and then Tara immediately opens it. What's the point of even knocking if she's going to just barge right in?

"C'mon lazy bum, we need to go shopping."

Tinley rolls over in bed and looks at the clock on her nightstand: it's not even nine yet. What the heck is her sister doing waking her up this early on a Saturday? "What are you even doing here, and what are you talking about?"

"It's an emergency. We need to get you a new outfit for your dates tonight."

Of course, because only Tara would be freaking out over something as inconsequential as a "fashion emergency." Tinley pulls her comforter over her head in hopes that it'll make her sister go away. When the cover is ripped from her face, she isn't the least bit surprised. She should have known it wasn't actually going to work. Her sister has always gotten her way. Even when they were kids, whatever Tara wanted, Tara got. Perks of being the first born she would have to guess.

"Yeah, about that...I'm not going."

Tara throws her arms up and places her hands on her hips. There's a scowl on her face as she rolls her eyes and her mom voice comes out, "Don't be ridiculous, of course you're going. We've already paid for it."

Well, she can't back out now. She'd feel guilty knowing they paid for the damn thing and she just skipped it—not that she asked them to do it or wants to go, but it'd still be a waste of money.

"Do you know how ridiculous you sound? The guy isn't going to be able to see me, and what do you mean by dates? As in plural?"

"It's not for the guys. If you have a cute outfit, you'll feel more confident and have a better time, and what did you think you were getting yourself into? We told you it was speed dating, meaning you'll have multiple dates."

"As long as that's all you mean and you didn't sign me up for multiple nights of this crap. Why do I let you two talk me into shit like this? Okay fine, if you're insistent on me getting new clothes, you're paying."

"Whatever, just get out of bed already. I'm limited on time. If I leave Livi with Clark for too long by himself, he goes a little crazy. That girl is too strong-willed, and her father doesn't know what to do with it."

She can't help but laugh at that. Livi is an exact replica of Tara. Tinley never understood why women would refer to their children as their mini-mes until her sister had her daughter. And that's precisely what Livi is. "What did he think he was getting into when he agreed to have children with you?"

"Trust me, I tell him the same thing every day."

They've been walking from store to store but Tara still isn't happy with anything they've come across, and Tinley won't even get started on the fact that this whole shopping trip seems to be about her sister and not her. Every time she tries to pick something up, Tara immediately puts it right back on the rack. Honestly, the whole excursion makes zero sense. Why make such a fuss about an outfit nobody else is going to see? Maybe it's the whole pregnancy thing—since she can't wear these cute clothes right now, she's picking out something for Tinley to wear now and she'll take it later for herself. Wouldn't be the first time Tara has "borrowed" something from Tinley's closet without asking.

After what seems like hours of walking in and out of stores, they've finally stumbled into one that has clothes her sister likes, and Tinley is just ready to get this day over with. The stack is growing steadily, and she just isn't mentally prepared for the disaster that is the fitting room. Tara grabs a tunic off the rack and looks it over. "How do you feel about sequins?"

"Whatever, just hand me what you have, and I'll try it all on." She reaches for the huge pile from Tara's hands. "Happy now?"

"Yep. Now get your cute butt into that fitting room and model everything for me."

With a huff, Tinley throws the pile of clothes over her shoulder and trudges her way over. She doesn't see an employee in sight when the rooms come into view and hopes she doesn't need a key to get in. She'd rather not have to drag herself all over the store with this ridiculous pile of clothing. She tries the first door in front of her, and of course, it's locked. The doors go all the way to the floor, so there's no way she can slide her body underneath even if she wanted to.

She starts to walk back out into the store when she spots a door slightly ajar at the end of the hallway. She shuffles past all the other rooms and pushes the door wide open. For a split second, she has that awkward panic moment—her feet glued to their spot on the floor and a look of horror on her face. She can't look away, but what's in front of her is absolutely terrifying.

The woman screams, which finally pulls Tinley out of her daze. She slams the door shut, the clothes tumble from her hands, and she hightails it out of there. She doesn't even stop to tell Tara she's leaving as she speed walks by her. The only thing on her mind is getting out of this store as fast as humanly possible without making a scene.

As soon as Tinley steps foot out of the store, someone pulls on her arm and whips her around. "What just happened? Why did you leave?"

Tinley tugs against Tara's grip and releases herself. She continues walking, not caring where she's going as long as it's far away from that store and that dressing room. "I just walked in on a woman in the dressing room."

"And?" Tara's hand goes down to her hip and the other rests on top of her belly. Sometimes Tinley wonders if she realizes she's doing it or if it's just instinct, mama bear mode automatically kicking in or something weird like that. She taps her foot and when Tinley doesn't say anything, she continues, "What's the big deal?"

"She was completely naked. She was trying to wiggle into a bathing suit that looked like it should be worn by a toddler. There was so little fabric and the hair...oh, my gosh, the hair. It was everywhere."

Tara rolls her eyes and lets out a huff. "What are you talking about?"

"I think she was one of those naturalists or something, you know, those people who don't believe in shaving their body hair? Well, her entire body was covered with super thick black curly hair. Super coarse pubic type hair. Come to think of it, that could have been a man in there. I don't know, I just saw all the hair, and it was painful." A shudder travels through Tinley's body as she tried to erase the mental image permanently branded on her brain. That shit is going to scar her for life.

Her voice gets louder near the end of her rant and a few people look over as they walk by. She didn't mean to draw a crowd, but she can't help how rough that whole situation was. She needs to bleach her eyes and stay in the shower all day long.

Tara is outright laughing, and Tinley can't tell whether or not she's laughing at her or with her. Either way, it's still embarrassing. "Do you realize how many times you just said the word hair? It couldn't have been that bad."

"You don't even know. I'm scarred for life. I might need therapy now. And you're paying for it because you forced me into this shopping trip in the first place."

"Okay drama queen, how about you save yourself the money, and we go grab a Frappuccino."

"Yeah, because caffeine is exactly what I need right now."

"They make those kiddie ones, vanilla bean or something like that, I think. Besides, I'm not drinking caffeine either, but I need something sweet. A large chocolate brownie or something."

They round the corner toward the coffee shop near the food court, and Tinley stops dead in her tracks. Standing at the counter is none other than Marek Outlaw. What are the odds? It's not like they have a lot of options for shopping in this area, just the one mall, but still, he doesn't really seem like a shopping mall kind of guy.

"What's going on? Why did you stop?"

Tinley's voice is caught in her throat as she tries to get the words out. Looking at him from this perspective, she can't deny how attractive he is. He's wearing a pair of dark jeans that hug him in all the right places. Fuck how did she never notice how amazing his ass is? And he has on a button-up with the sleeves rolled up. *Hello, arm candy.* She never knew she could be attracted to a forearm before, but Marek has fantastic forearms.

She's practically panting as she licks her lips and turns toward her sister. "The guy standing at the counter right now is Marek Outlaw."

"Oh, the jackhole you work with?" Tara's attention turns toward the counter where Marek is still standing, and her eyes practically bug out of her head. "Holy shit he's good-looking—like straight out of GQ good-looking. If I weren't madly in love with Clark, I would totally consider throwing my marriage away for a night alone with that guy. How do you get any work done with him in the same room?"

"It's easy: he's a giant jerk. He's a gorgeous jerk, but a jerk nonetheless. Why don't we go somewhere else?"

"Don't be such a baby. I need a sugar fix, and this is the only place in the mall where you can get baked goods. It's not like we have to say hi to him or anything."

Tinley begrudgingly follows her sister into the shop, and they join the line. As Marek finishes his order, it doesn't take him long to spot the two of them standing at the back of the very long line. Their eyes instantly meet, and Tinley's heart rate picks up as he walks closer to them. The connection between them is strong, and she almost steps out of line to get closer to him. What the heck is going on with her?

He nears her, and his voice is only slightly above a whisper as he breathes out, "Tinley."

She almost swoons right there on the spot, but her sister interrupts her thoughts. "Hi, I'm Tara, Tinley's sister."

He reaches his hand out and shakes hers. "Marek. Tinley and I work together."

"Oh, so you're the famous Marek." Tinley whips her head to the side and watches as her sister smiles a big bold smile then she switches her focus to Marek, who has the sexiest smirk on his face.

"So, you've heard of me? All good things I hope?"

Tara laughs and shakes her head. "No, I was totally kidding. I just like embarrassing my little sister here any chance I can get."

As they continue their conversation, a tall woman sidles up next to Marek and hands him a cup. She's got jet-black hair that falls down her back and has an exotic Victoria's Secret supermodel look to her. She smiles and sizes up both Tinley and Tara.

Awkward.

"Tinley, Tara, this is—"

She possessively wraps her arms around Marek's middle and smiles in that wicked claiming-my-man kind of way as she says, "I'm Giselle."

Even her voice is sexy in a sultry *I've smoked a pack of cigarettes every day of my life* way, with that low rasp Tinley would kill to have rather than the childlike voice of a twelve-year-old that she actually does have. Some women just have all the luck.

The silence becomes uncomfortably awkward as they all just stand there staring at each other. Tinley doesn't know whether or not she should say something or just let the silence continue, but she chooses to do the latter. Her sister is unusually quiet as well, probably enjoying how uncomfortable Tinley is getting. Awkward silences always make her nervous.

"Well, it was nice seeing you both. See you at work on Monday, Tinley." Marek pulls himself from the claws wrapped around his arm and walks out of the coffee shop. The conversation between him and Giselle seems to be very heated, which makes the whole situation even weirder.

"That was weird, right?"

"The fact that she was claiming her territory? I mean, we're not hideous, so not really that weird at all—although I am very pregnant, so I don't think she was too worried about me." Tara adds that last bit with a wink.

Yeah, because the gorgeous woman standing in front of them would have anything to worry about. There's no competition. Tinley has an extra fifty pounds she's been trying to lose for nearly a decade, and she didn't get lucky in the looks department. She'd describe herself as average at best. And that woman? She probably has a line of men throwing themselves at her feet. Even her name is gorgeous. Giselle.

Tinley shakes her head and says, "No, that's not what I meant. He just seemed really uncomfortable about the whole thing. I've never known Marek to be uncomfortable about anything."

"I don't know, some people are just different outside of work than they are when they're at work. That's probably all it was."

"Maybe."

But Tinley didn't think so. There was definitely something weird about the way Marek was acting. She just can't figure out what that is.

FIVE

Tinley's sweaty palms slip on her steering wheel as she turns the corner, pulling into the parking lot next to the restaurant. Her nerves are through the roof, but more than anything, she's mad. Why did she give in to something as stupid as this? Those bitches—the audacity to say she was in need of this? Just because her thirtieth birthday is right around the corner doesn't mean she has some kind of biological clock ticking away. Plenty of women focus on their careers and then worry about settling down later. That's actually become the norm, although if Tinley were being honest with herself, she doesn't really have much to show for her almost thirty years of life. What does she have? An extra fifty pounds that she could work toward losing but loves cupcakes way too much to part with, a dead-end job selling cruise packages to people over the phone though she's never even been on a cruise herself, and to top it all off, she lives with her best friend because said job doesn't pay her well enough to afford the rent on her own.

Yeah, Tinley, your life is looking really promising and exciting, and—ugh—a cupcake sounds really good right about now. She still has a couple from her last batch of strawberries and cream waiting for her at home. Her mouth salivates just thinking about the burst of flavor from the juicy strawberries. Not to mention the chocolate espresso ones she made last night still need to be frosted. Tara's little shopping trip interrupted her plans of doing that today. The cold metal of the gear shift meets her fingertips as she considers backing her car right up and driving home.

A tapping on her window causes her to jump in her seat and scream as she sees a smiling face looking back at her. *What in the actual fuck?* The excessively perky blonde does a small finger wave, and Tinley reluctantly lowers her window. Her senses are overwhelmed by a disgustingly sweet floral scent as Barbie widens her smile.

Her voice is overly peppy, and Tinley silently wonders if she used to be a cheerleader? "Hi there. Are you here for Dating in the Dark?"

Now is her chance. All she has to do is say no and turn right back around toward the comfort of her home and delicious cupcakes. Dakota said she wasn't going to be home at all tonight so no one would ever know...but Tinley would know. She would feel the weight of guilt as soon as the cupcake hit the pit of her stomach, and there's no way she could lie to her sister or Dakota if they asked how tonight went—scratch that, *when* they ask because they both will.

Screw it. Her signature call center smile goes up, and she says, "Yeah, looks like I am. This is my first time, so not really sure what to expect."

Blondie's entire face lights up, and she checks something off on the clipboard she's holding. "Oh, yay! I'm so happy you're here with us. I was just coming out to round up any stragglers. We're looking to get started in about five minutes, and I just wanted to let you know. And don't worry. It's totally not scary at all. Do you have any questions before you come inside?"

Why the hell are you organizing something as stupid as this? Will stabbing myself in the eye with a fork be more exciting than what I'm about to participate in? Are you single too? Am I at risk of being murdered when I step foot in that restaurant? Do you run background checks on the people who sign up for this or can anyone just come in off the street as long as they have the cash to drop? "Nope, not that I can think of."

"Okay perfect. Well, I'll see you inside in a few then." She walks away toward a group of women walking through the parking lot, and her very perky voice carries back to Tinley. If there's one thing that woman doesn't have an issue with, it's projecting her voice. "Hey ladies, are you here for Dating in the Dark?"

Does she have to fill a quota or something? Or maybe

they have situations where people sign up and then never show up. That would be kind of awkward to have people waiting on the sidelines...unless they have to turn those people away, so everyone has a date the entire time. To be honest, the whole thing sounds kind of stressful, but then again, Tinley was never one for the whole party-planning thing. She was in charge of organizing an event in high school once, and it didn't go over well. By the end, she wanted to pull all of her hair out and murder her entire team. Luckily, she didn't do either.

Begrudgingly, she gets out of her car and slides her still sweaty palms down the front of her dress. After the shopping trip ended up being a disaster, Tinley stole something from Dakota's closet. The dress hugs her in all the "right" places, but Tinley is the furthest thing from comfortable right now. Part of that is due to the Spanx sucking all of her extra baggage in. She takes one small step, and her heel gets caught in a crack in the concrete. *Just great.* She has all the luck in the world. She goes to take another step, but her heel won't budge, and she's stuck in place. Adding a little more force to her stride, she tugs and hears the one sound she doesn't want to hear. The heel cracks and she falls down due to the momentum, leaving the heel of Dakota's shoe completely broken.

Her ass is the first thing down on the asphalt, and the impact sends a shockwave through her body. She cries out in pain, and the skin on both of her palms is skinned from where she tried to break her fall. She looks around and fortunately, no one was around to witness her misery, but now she's really tempted to get up and go home. If her klutziness is any indication of how the evening is going to go, it's a disaster waiting to happen. Regaining her composure, she slips both heels off her feet and stands up not so gracefully. She tugs on the heel still stuck in the pavement, and magically it comes right out; she probably should have just taken the shoe off in the first place. Tossing all the pieces into the trunk of her car, she pulls out her trusty Chucks and slides them on. Good thing she doesn't have to impress anyone with her outfit.

She hobbles toward the restaurant trying to go as fast as possible. But with each step, her ass screams in pain. That is going to leave one nasty bruise that is for sure. She can already feel the size of it growing. Hopefully, it isn't too bad because she has to sit on her butt for the next hour and being in physical pain will just make this whole night that much worse. When she makes her way inside, she is kind of shocked at the turnout. The tables in the middle of the room are completely empty, but the walls are lined with at least thirty different women. She thought for sure this whole thing would be a bust, but it looks like she was very wrong.

Tinley glances around the room, and for the most part, everyone looks normal, but if there's one thing she has learned from her job at the call center, it's that looks can be deceiving. She swears most of the old ladies with the foulest mouths are probably the sweetest-looking ones in person. Everyone is hiding something, and you definitely can't always judge a book by its cover—except for the busty blonde in the corner. Her hair is bigger than the state of Texas, her top is cut all the way down to her belly, and Tinley can just imagine the cloud of perfume floating off of her right now. She's definitely not hiding anything unless of course, she stashed it in her hair; then who knows what she's got concealed.

The unassuming redhead standing next to Miss Texas looks like a librarian. She's wearing a dull colored cardigan, an ill-fitting pencil skirt, and a pair of Mary Jane's on her feet. Her outward appearance is the epitome of boring, but if Tinley had to guess on the kink scale from one to ten, this woman is definitely an eleven.

Well, maybe they're not all so normal. Off in the corner, there's a woman standing all by herself. She's got mousy brown hair and is wearing some crazy leggings that are covered in cats, which matches perfectly with her oversized sequined tunic that has a giant cat in the middle. Yep, that one is a crazy cat lady for sure.

She continues her judgment of the "competition" and finds herself rather entertained making up potential stories about each of their lives. There's the single mom with the bags under her eyes, the perky sorority girl who is probably also a cheerleader, the surgical intern who is looking for a night off but keeps looking at her phone every time a beep goes off in the room, the former beauty queen turned stripper, and so on. She has a story for almost every woman in the room when the door from outside opens up.

The blonde from outside comes in a few seconds later

with her clipboard in hand. She closes the door to the room and steps in the middle, calling everyone's attention to her. "I want to thank you all for joining us tonight for Dating in the Dark. It should be a really fun evening, and we're just about ready to get started. First off, I'm going to have you all take a seat at the tables. Please sit on the far side of the table facing toward the door. Your dates will all be seated across from you."

She pauses and motions for everyone to start moving. The click-clacking of heels echoes throughout the room as they all make their way to the various tables. Tinley takes a seat at one farthest from the door and patiently waits for the woman to continue explaining everything.

"Perfect, now that you're all seated, the waiters are going to file into the room and take your drink orders. Once you're all set, we'll get started."

Surprisingly, the whole drink ordering and delivery process takes a lot less time than Tinley expected. Each table has their own waiter assigned to them, so it runs rather smoothly. Maybe this whole night won't be so bad after all.

"Okay ladies, we're going to go grab the guys and let the fun begin. Just remember, we're keeping this one hundred percent confidential, so on top of not being able to see each other, no sharing names either, okay? Okay, well you all have fun! Happy dating." Then the lights are cut, and Tinley is surrounded by nothing but darkness.

What have I gotten myself into?

SIX

The fact that they're in a pitch-black room is supposed to add to the mystery, but for Tinley, all it does is make the situation that much more unnerving. The creaking of a door being opened somewhere only adds to her unease. Any minute now, one of those guys will be sitting in the chair across from her, and the weight of dread in the pit of her stomach intensifies. As the sound of many feet shuffles into the room, she slides her hand across the cold metal of the tabletop in front of her. Luckily, they provided them with drinks ahead of time, but now she's questioning her choice of getting a glass of wine instead of a cocktail. The extra alcohol content might have helped her nerves a little bit more.

Nevertheless, she takes a small sip and then another.

The tart apples and crisp pears dance together on her tongue and slide effortlessly down her throat. She's had a lot of wine in her life, but this one is exceptionally refreshing. If the wine is any indication, she's about ready to enjoy a pretty fantastic meal. Not judging at all on the dates. But who knows, maybe it won't be so bad after all.

The familiar sound of a wooden chair scraping against concrete perks her ears up as her first date takes his seat at the table. She was so wrapped up in the wine, she didn't even notice that some of the dates at the tables around her had already started. *Way to pay attention, Tinley.*

"Hey, what's going on?" asks the voice from across the table at an obnoxiously loud level. Maybe it's the disorientation of being in the dark and not realizing that even though they can't see each other, she can hear him just fine.

Tinley laughs and replies to the stranger at a much lower volume, "Oh, you know, not much at all. This is—"

She jumps as the entire table shakes with what she can only assume is his hand slamming down on it. "Obviously I don't know, or I wouldn't ask. Why do women always insist on expecting us to be mind readers? You could just tell us what you want, and then we would know."

Is this guy for real right now?

She doesn't have a chance to contemplate that for long because the waiter stops by their table with their first course. "I hope you're both enjoying your evening so far."

There's a brief pause, and she knows he's waiting for an answer, but neither one of them speak up. "Okay, well, I've brought your first course for the evening. It's a crusted—"

"Just leave the food so we can get on with it. I don't need to know every single detail about the food going into my mouth. If you guys fucked it up, I can just get a refund."

Man, this guy has some serious anger issues. Makes her wonder why he even came to this event in the first place. Maybe he got roped into it like she did, but she'd be surprised if anyone were able to convince this guy to do anything. He seriously seems like a major dick with a capital D. Must be trying to compensate for the lack of down south.

The plate is placed before her and her mouth waters at the scents trickling up to her nose. Silverware clatters against the plates around the small room, and audible moans and groans travel throughout.

"Enjoy your meal," the waiter adds before quickly walking away. *Yeah buddy, I'd be going along with you right now if I could.*

The cold metal of the fork meets her hand as Tinley picks it up and takes a bite of her food. The flavors explode on impact, and the crab melts on her tongue. The combination of the sip of wine she just tasted and the crab salad work perfectly together, and she's glad she decided to go with the Pinot Grigio after all.

She welcomes the silence as they both dig into their

food. It's only after the chatter around them alarms her to the wasted date she's currently on that she opens her mouth to attempt to salvage the date by asking what he thought of the dish, but before she even has a chance to get a word out, his rant starts right back up again. "Do you know how much easier all this dating bullshit would be if everyone was honest with each other? I mean seriously, what's with the games? I don't need another tease making me buy her a bunch of drinks when I get dick in return. Like, what the fuck? This shit is getting old."

Tease making him buy her a bunch of drinks? What is this dude even talking about? He's not paying for any of her meal. Somebody has definitely burned this guy a time or two before. He's harboring way too much anger and just throwing it at a stranger. Maybe since he can't actually see her, he doesn't care about what he's saying? She continues working her way through her salad and enjoys every last bite of it.

As she clears her plate and wipes off her mouth, she takes another sip of wine and gathers her thoughts. "I have no idea what your deal is or why you're even here since you're so clearly not enjoying it, but I'd appreciate if you would calm yourself down. This is unnecessary."

"Oh, the princess is going to have a fit. Well, sorry to break it to you bitch, but I'm not your knight in shining armor. No one is here to save you right now. And if you came here searching for a fucking prince, then you're even more pathetic than I gave you credit for."

Tinley opens her mouth to tell him off but is saved by

the ringing of the bell. She breathes a tiny sigh of relief that things didn't escalate further. She was a little worried about the direction that date was taking. Date one down, three more to go. It can't really get any worse than this one, can it?

SEVEN

The crackling of a speaker spreads around the room as the same woman from earlier talks over a PA system. "Okay everyone, your first dates are done. Guys, please get up and move to the next chair on your right. Once everyone is seated, your waiters will come by to remove the first course plates and serve the second course."

Tinley lets out an internal sigh of relief. Her "date" gets up from the table without another word, and she's very grateful that he's someone else's problem for the next fifteen minutes. That's awful of her to think, but at least he's out of her hair for the time being. Now on to the next date. If anything, she just hopes it doesn't get any worse. She doesn't have high hopes for a spectacular date, but someone who doesn't spend the next fifteen minutes screaming at her would be nice.

The clattering of dishes alerts her to the fact that the waiter is back at her table. The polite thing to do would be to thank him for clearing everything away, but she obviously can't see anything and wouldn't even know which direction she should be facing.

"Here, I brought you a refill. I thought you might need one after that last guy."

She jumps slightly at the closeness of the voice. She had no idea the waiter was still at her table, but she did, in fact, finish off her last glass before the end of that debacle. "Thank you so much. I appreciate it."

"No problem. Hope your next one isn't as bad." With that, she hears the familiar shuffling as he walks away.

That's precisely what she's hoping for as well. At this point, if she makes it through the night unscathed, she'll consider it a success. How pathetic is that? And even though she didn't even want to come to this thing, she had a tiny morsel of hope that she would find a decent guy. She doesn't need a man to define her, but having some companionship of the male variety would be nice for a change.

The chair across from her scrapes on the floor again, and Tinley doesn't even let this guy sit down before laying into him. "Before we even get started, I need to know if you're in need of anger management or if you've ever been arrested for assault."

A deep chuckle travels across the table to her and he asks, "Can't say that I have. Bad breakup or something?"

She contemplates that for half a second. She's been with a lot of assholes in her life, but none of them have been outright violent or scary. And she's definitely never dated anyone who had a record.

"Nope. The first guy went psycho on me. I was a little afraid he might flip the table or something."

There's a long pause, and she's almost tempted to ask him if he's still there...although if he isn't there, she wouldn't really be asking him, but an empty chair. An empty chair could be better than her current date; jury's still out on that one. *Ugh.* She's getting a little too introspective tonight; might need to start pacing herself on the wine, at least until more food arrives.

"Seriously? That's intense."

"Right? Honestly, I don't even know why I'm here right now."

He doesn't miss a beat as he whips right back at her, "Then why are you here?"

"My sister and roommate signed me up. They kind of forced me to come, so here I am."

Their conversation is interrupted as the waiter comes by with the second course. After that salad, she's hoping the yummy food keeps on coming.

"And now I have your second course for the evening. On your plate, you'll find a trio of stuffed mushrooms. The first one is filled with a seafood combination of oysters and scallops, the second one has an Italian sausage filling, and finally, the third has a variety of cheeses inside."

Tinley's mouth starts salivating as her plate is placed

in front of her. Cheese is one of her many weaknesses, and the air around her is filling with the smell of the melted goodness. She's dying to dig right in.

"Nah bro, you can take mine away. I don't eat anything that comes from the ocean. You can't trust that stuff."

Not a seafood fan? This guy just lost points in Tinley's book for that response. She might be a food lover in general, hence the extra fifty pounds, but seafood is like heaven in food form. If it wasn't so damn expensive, she'd eat sushi for dinner every night.

"Not a problem sir. Is there anything else I can get for you?"

"Yeah, dude. Can you refill my Bud? That would be most excellent."

"Of course. And for you, miss?"

"I'm good, thank you," Tinley replies, and she can just imagine the amusement her waiter is having this evening. Her dates aren't living up to any kind of potential, but at least she's providing some entertainment for the staff.

He jumps right back into the conversation like they were never interrupted. "Are they hot?"

"Um, excuse me?" Tinley asks as she coughs into her napkin.

"Are they hot? You know, we could take this party back to your place and have a little fun of the naked variety, if you know what I mean."

She imagines the dude winking with that last comment. Who even asks something like that? "I'm not an idiot, so of course I know what you mean, but what part of that sounded like a good idea when it came out of your mouth?"

"All of it?"

"How old are you?"

"Twenty-one. Why does that matter?"

"I'm not sure what kind of porn fantasy you're trying to create here, but not now and not ever will I get naked and do anything sexual with my sister or my roommate."

"Whoa babe, cool your jets. Can't blame a guy for trying."

Tinley is once again saved by the ringing bell. She was about five seconds away from jumping over the table and throttling his neck. Don't they do any kind of vetting on these people? Where are the normal guys at? Oh, that's right, all the good ones her age are married and have kids. They're at home with their families right now while Tinley is polishing off yet another glass of wine in the dark. At this rate, she'll have to take a taxi home.

She places her glass back down on the table and thinks, *Bring on the next one.*

EIGHT

Tinley jumps as a voice speaks to her from across the table. She didn't even hear the chair move or her new date sit down.

"Do you have a hand I can shake? I promise not to bite you. I'm not a vampire, so I'm not into that kind of thing."

That's not the kind of response she was expecting in the least. Maybe this date will be a little fun after all. Playing along, she reaches her hand across the table, feeling for his. "Not a vampire, huh? That's too bad—I hear that can be kind of hot."

Just as their fingertips touch, he rips his hand away from hers and exclaims, "Oh no! Not in the slightest. It's very dangerous. I almost lost a friend to a vampire once. I was able to give him a blood transfusion and he survived, though just barely. It's the females you need to worry about. They're brutal."

What the fuck? Do normal people not come to this kind of thing? *Of course not, Tinley.* Who in their right mind would willingly go to something called Dating in the Dark? The answer is nobody would, and she's stuck here with those nobodies for at least another thirty minutes.

All communication stops as the waiter brings by their main course. She doesn't pay attention to a word he says about what they're eating because her mind can't get off the fact that this guy thinks vampires are real. Of course, she's wondered what life would be like if supernatural creatures were real and that world would have to include Dean and Sam, but she's never for one minute thought that was reality. They're just made-up stories.

"So, what species are you?"

She chokes as she takes a small sip of her wine. Maybe she needs to switch to water and stop drinking the wine because she obviously heard him wrong. *Species*— what kind of question is that? She clears her throat after a few too many coughs and croaks out, "Um, human?"

"Hm...a humanoid...how...predictable." He takes long pauses in between his words and drags them all out. It almost sounds like he's having trouble breathing, but maybe that's just how he talks? He's either longwinded or only speaks in staccato.

Predictable? What part of any of this is predictable? It's hard to imagine that anything would shock this guy at this point. "I'm sorry?"

DATING *in the* DARK

"No need to be sorry—you can't change what you are. I shouldn't have expected much coming to this thing, but you're my third date and only humanoids so far. I think I'm going about this whole dating thing the wrong way. I just don't know where to meet other people, you know?"

At this point, the only obvious conclusion is that she needs to humor this guy; at least then she'll have a good story to tell her sister and Dakota. They'll never believe she went on a date with a guy who thinks he's an alien. "So, if you aren't a human, what are you?"

"My people...call themselves...the Vikkulas. I come from...the planet...Eplora."

Wow, this guy is actually serious. Like full-blown believes every word that he's saying kind of crazy. "I've never heard of that before. Is it far away? How did you get here?"

"Well...if I told you...any of that...I'd have to...kill you. Then they'd know...I was here."

She starts to laugh, but he interrupts her.

"I'm serious. You can't tell anyone what I've told you. If anyone found out, it would be dangerous for both of us. The consequences would be dire, and my whole planet and race would be at risk."

"Then why did you just tell me all that? We don't even know each other."

The bell rings signaling the end of their date, and Tinley is almost sad to see this one go. He's batshit crazy, that's for sure, but the story he was telling was just so fascinating, and she could tell he believed every word coming out of his mouth. How else do you explain someone who has a species and planet name at the ready? Maybe he's a writer or an actor and was testing out a storyline? Either way, she could never be that creative.

As the guys get up and start shuffling around the room again, her friend the waiter stops by to clear their dinner plates, and she only just now realizes she didn't even touch a bite of whatever was on there. So much for that. "So, how did date number three go?"

"Alien."

There's a long pause as he stops clearing away the dishes and coughs. "Come again?"

That is the normal reaction to this situation: complete and utter shock mixed with some confusion. She almost wishes she could follow him around to all of his dates and hear their reactions. It's not every day you go on a date with an alien. Now that would be some entertainment right there.

"The guy thought he was an alien, gave me this whole spiel about keeping his secret because the government would come after him and me. Where do these people even come from?"

"Your guess is as good as mine. Who knows, maybe the next guy will be a winner, or maybe you'll consider letting me take you out sometime."

"That's very sweet of you, but no offense, I don't think I want to see anyone from tonight a second time. This whole night has been a giant disaster."

"Hey, I get it, but sometimes you just need to find a

silver lining. So, in case you change your mind, I'm leaving a napkin here with my phone number on it. No pressure."

He walks away and she feels around the table for the napkin. After a split-second decision, she shoves it into her purse. Who knows, maybe she'll get a wild hair and decide to text the guy. More than likely it'll end up in the trash as soon as she gets home, but it doesn't hurt to take it just in case she changes her mind, and now she's ready for her last date of the evening.

Bring it on.

NINE

As the seconds tick by, Tinley contemplates her current predicament. She could get up now and not sit through another atrocious date, or she could finish the evening, gain another five pounds from the chocolate concoction sitting in front of her, suffer through the last date, and be done with it. She weighs the pros and cons of her choice for far too long and the chair across from her scrapes along the floor. The hairs on the back of her neck go up and she cringes while feeling around the table for her fork. Might as well dig in while she's still got the chance. Who knows what kind of disaster is in store. She takes a giant bite of the chocolate lava brownie and it immediately melts on her tongue. The combination of cookie dough chunks mixed in with the rich molten syrup flowing down over the dessert is enough to put her in a sugar coma.

She reaches for another bite as her date sits down in the seat across from her. "Hey, I'm—shit, sorry. I keep forgetting about the no names thing. You'd think by now I would know better. I'm your last date for the evening."

Tinley's ears perk up at the sound of his voice; it's super low and incredibly sexy. She feels along the table for her glass of wine and takes a large gulp of liquid courage before responding. "That's okay, I've always been a fan of rule-breakers. Some rules were just meant to be broken. For now, I'll just call you Mystery Date Number Four."

A husky chuckle floats across the table, and she can't help but be instantly attracted. She can't see his face, but with a voice like that, it doesn't even matter what he looks like. "Is that because I'm your fourth date or are you ranking us? What's my competition look like?"

All thoughts of being ladylike go out the window as Tinley lets out a full-blown belly laugh. If this guy only knew. "If by ranking, you mean which date was the worst, it's hard to tell at this point."

"Is that so? I had some pretty bad ones myself."

She laughs internally at the disastrous dates she's had so far. There's no way he can compete. "I don't know, my dates were pretty awful. I don't think you can top them."

"You want to bet?"

"Oh, we're making bets now? I guess our relationship

just cranked up a notch. Instead of it just being a blind date, we're now at the blind acquaintance level."

She's not sure where this level of confidence came from, but she's liking how easily the conversation is flowing with this guy. It's completely effortless and she's just comfortable. It's never been this way with anyone before.

"Is that a thing?"

"It is now." She finds herself nodding along as she answers until she remembers he can't actually see her.

"Fair enough."

"How about we go back and forth and find out who truly had the worst dates?"

"I'm game, but I've got to warn you, mine were pretty bad."

We'll see about that. Hers went from bad to worse. "My first date, the guy had anger management issues, as in screamed at me from the very beginning and wouldn't even let me get a single word in."

"That's pretty bad, but the woman I had for my first date wanted to call me 'daddy' and kept asking me to spank her."

"Without seeing your face? I get being into some kinky stuff, but don't you have to trust the person you're doing it with first?"

"Apparently not. Now c'mon, spill on the second date."

"Oh, that guy was a real winner. He was twenty-one, pretty sure he was a frat guy, and he wanted to have a four-way with himself, me, my sister, and my roommate."

His laugh surrounds her, and she just wants to wrap herself up in it.

"I need to know, how did that discussion come about?"

"They're the ones who signed me up for this and it just came out, and I guess to college boy, that's an invitation to bring them to the bedroom. So gross."

"Yeah, that's a little weird. My second one wasn't all that weird, just a crazy cat lady."

She knows exactly which woman he's referring to; it wasn't very hard to peg her as a cat lover based on everything she was wearing. "There always has to be at least one in the bunch. My last date, he definitely takes the cake. He told me he was an alien from another planet, had a whole story about the name of his people and the planet he comes from."

"You're right, you win. I can't top that at all. Where do these people even come from? Do they just suddenly come out of the woodwork for shit like this?"

She can't just win because he says she wins; that's boring, and she's such a snoop. She has to know what actually happened. "C'mon, you have to tell me. What happened on your last date?"

"It was pretty uneventful. We got two minutes into the date and she got up and left. She didn't say anything either. So, I couldn't tell you if she went to the bathroom or if I got a complete brushoff."

"You're right, I totally win." Even if she won in the sucky date category, everything is looking up with her current date. At least they are having a conversation together—it's more than she can say about the other guys.

The bell rings for the fourth and final time for the evening and Tinley's shoulders drop. She is actually enjoying herself on this date and doesn't want it to end. They didn't really get to know each other, but the conversation was flowing easily and they had a fun banter going on. Who knew something like that would happen?

"It was nice meeting you. Maybe I'll be hearing from you again soon."

"Yeah, it was good meeting you as well."

Her shoulders slump forward even more. That was a brushoff if she's ever heard one. No point in trying to get this guy's number after that.

"Okay everyone, thank you all for coming. We're going to have all the guys leave the room and then we'll turn the lights back on. We'll have everyone fill out a comment card with the date you'd like to see again. If there are any matches, you'll each get the other's phone number."

It doesn't take long for the guys to leave the room, and suddenly everyone is blinded as the lights come back on. It takes a few minutes as Tinley blinks over and over, but finally, her eyes adjust. Looking down, she finds the comment card that was just mentioned and grabs the pen lying next to it.

She quickly fills in the information about her fourth date, but doubt starts to set in. What if he doesn't want to see her again and she waits around to be told that? Rather than risking rejection, she quickly fills it out, writes in her permission for him to be given her phone number, and drops it off at the table at the front of the room. Only time will tell if he actually reaches out or not.

TEN

*A*nother start to another week, but after how this weekend went, Tinley's feeling a little less manic this Monday morning. She actually woke up smiling, and that is definitely a first. For once in her life, she's feeling pleasantly optimistic. She has no idea whether or not her last date will reach out to her, but she's crossing her fingers that he does so they can continue getting to know one another.

"So, you never told me how it went on Saturday. You have to tell me everything."

It went amazingly. It was wonderful. It was one of the best dates Tinley has ever been on. She shrugs and mumbles, "It was okay. There are definitely some crazy people out there."

"You've got that right." Dakota finishes typing up an

email and then hits send. "So, was it a complete bust, or was there anyone there that could have potential?"

She contemplates that for a minute. Mystery guy number four was amazing. She's pretty sure she could easily fall in love with a guy like him and they'd make gorgeous babies and live happily ever after. The only problem is that it seemed like it was going great until he got dismissive at the end. Knowing her track record, she'll never hear from him again. "You tell me. Which guy should I go on a second date with? The one with anger management issues, the twenty-year-old frat boy who wants to have an orgy with you, Tara, and myself, or the alien who also believes in vampires? I'm pretty partial to that last one, but I'm not really sure how that would work out. I mean, do aliens even have penises?"

Dakota starts coughing like crazy and takes a giant sip of her coffee before turning back toward Tinley. "Say that again? One of the guys actually told you he was alien?"

"Oh yeah. He told me he was an alien and warned me off of vampires. I had dates with a bunch of real winners."

She's still laughing as hard as she can which of course has disturbed the few people sitting around them. She stops long enough to say, "I'm sorry. That sounds hilarious, but I'm sorry it was a bust and little Tinley won't be getting any extra attention any time soon."

"Domestic," the whisper says, alerting Tinley to a new call coming in, and she puts her finger up to let Dakota know it will be a moment and her roommate turns back to her own computer.

For the millionth time since she started this job, the idea of quitting crosses her mind. She doesn't enjoy the work and yet she's been doing it for five years now. The entire routine and robotic aspect of this job just bores her. She needs to figure out what it is she actually wants to do with her life because she can't stay here until she retires, that's for sure. She plasters on her fake smile and says, "Thank you for calling Wanderlust International, my name is Tinley, can I cure your lust for adventure with a European cruise today?"

Sometimes she likes to mix it up and not always push the Caribbean cruises. She's never sold a European cruise before, but the bonus check on one of those would pay half of her month's rent, so it's always worth a shot.

There's a cough on the other end and the guy mumbles out, "Um...yeah...let's do one of those Europe cruise thingies."

Her heart rate speeds up as she gets excited at the thought of finally booking one. The smile on her face has completely transformed from fake to real. She pulls up a list of itineraries and starts right in. "Perfect. I can definitely help you out with that sir. When would you like to travel? And do you have an idea of which countries you'd like to visit?"

There's a long pause and Tinley has to look down at her phone to make sure the call is still connected. After a full minute, he comes back and says, "Well, ya know...I'm not really sure. To be honest, I haven't really thought much about that part."

Weird. Red flags are going up, but Tinley decides to push forward and give this guy the benefit of the doubt. Maybe he has a lot of places he wants to see and needs ideas. So, she changes tactics with her line of questioning. "Is there a special reason you're planning a trip? Or are you just getting the itch to travel?"

Again, there's a long pause on the other end, but fortunately, this one doesn't last quite as long. "Oh, um, I'm planning on proposing to my girlfriend."

Well, hopefully you're a little more assertive with the proposal than you are with planning this trip.

"What was that?"

What was what? "I'm not sure what you mean, sir."

The voice on the other end of the line comes back a lot more forceful, and his entire persona changes. "I'm sorry my social anxiety is causing you issues. This is a big step for me and just thinking about it makes me nervous, but if you need a more assertive customer, maybe I should give this sale to someone else. Transfer me to a supervisor now. I don't want to have this conversation with you anymore."

No! That did not just happen. She was thinking those thoughts, but did she actually say them out loud and to a customer? She feels completely defeated as the reality of what just happened sets in. So much for thinking about quitting this job—she's probably about to get fired. "One moment sir." She mutes her phone and hits the transfer button to the supervisor line. She immediately puts her phone into *do not disturb* mode and turns to her roommate. "Holy shit. Dakota!"

"Yeah?"

Her roommate continues typing away while Tinley is having a mental breakdown. Her fingers tap on her keyboard and all Tinley can ask is, "What have I done?"

That gets a little attention from her and she looks away from her screen but continues typing. "Okay drama queen, what's going on now?"

What is going on now? She got cocky and stopped paying full attention to what she was saying to her customer. Just because she had one good date doesn't mean she's suddenly invincible. This is not the kind of person she has ever been and she has no idea what just happened. The entire conversation plays over and over in her head like a broken record. This right here will be her downfall. Years from now when she's locked up in a padded room, they'll be able to trace it back to this day.

Any minute now she'll be getting fired and the conversation she just had will haunt her. She'll wake up screaming every night as she continues repeating this moment over and over when she goes to sleep. It'll be enough to drive her mad. All because she had a measly date that distracted her from what's important. She is so incredibly screwed. She opens her mouth to start recounting the conversation when she's interrupted.

"Tinley, can I speak to you for a moment?"

Shit. This is not good. Her entire face heats up and she stares down at the keyboard in front of her. When she transferred the call, apparently Marek was the one who picked it up. Now he's going to drag her to their boss's office, the dude who runs the whole freaking call center, and he will fire her right on the spot. This is not good at all.

"Why are you over here Marek? This whole power trip thing you've got going on is super unattractive. It's not like you supervise either one of us, so you really have no reason to be over here."

"Cut the attitude, Dakota. I'm talking to Tinley, and I'm pretty sure she can speak for herself."

"Are you kidding—"

She needs to stop this. All Dakota is doing is making the whole situation worse. Tinley got herself into this mess and now she needs to go face the consequences, no matter how bad they may be.

"It's fine Dakota, just stop." She gets up from her chair and is completely surprised when Marek leads her outside rather than to the department manager's office. She follows him over to the bench in the smoking area, and surprisingly, it's empty for once.

He takes a seat and looks up at her. "You want to tell me what happened?"

"Not really." She takes a seat next to him and mumbles out, "I feel like such an idiot right now."

"I'm not going to pretend like we're friends. We barely even talk, but is there something going on in your personal life that has you distracted?"

All she can do is nod, and her eyes turn down to the

ground. This whole situation is so embarrassing.

"I covered for you this time, but I don't want it to happen again."

Her eyes go wide as her focus switches from the ground to his face. "You did what?"

"I apologized to the customer and explained that your desk is right next to the break room, so he probably heard a combination of conversations in the background. I said you would never say something like what he heard. I also explained to him that I would have a conversation with you about it and we would see about moving you away from that location so something like this wouldn't happen again. I did end up salvaging the sale and booking the trip, so I took the commission on it."

Is he serious right now? She jumps up and wraps her arms around his neck in a tight hug. "Oh my gosh! Thank you! I don't even care about the commission. Five seconds ago, I thought I was going to get fired. My bigger concern was still having a job."

His entire body is stiff and he coughs slightly, reminding her that she is, in fact, hugging him. *Oops, might have gone a little overboard.* She releases her hold on him and mouths, "Sorry."

He steps back and runs his hand along the back of his neck. "It's fine, it's just not very professional. So, we're good, right?"

She nods enthusiastically. "We're perfect, and I won't ever let that happen again, I promise. Thank you again, so much!"

"Tinley, I know we give each other shit all the time, and I can be a dick, but that doesn't mean I want to see someone lose their job. So, if you've got something going on that's distracting you outside of work get it figured out because next time I won't be able to cover for you."

She nods slowly unable to think of a coherent response to offer him. She has no idea what she did to deserve Marek being a decent human being for once, but she's not going to push her luck by asking why he's being so nice.

"Unless you have anything else to say, I think we're done here. You should probably get back to your station."

"Absolutely." She hurries back inside before he suddenly decides to change his mind. She's almost breathless as she makes it back to her desk and takes a seat.

"So, you want to tell me what all that was about?"

She shrugs, puts her headset back on, and unlocks her monitor. "Honestly, I don't even know. One minute I thought I was going to get fired and the next Marek decided to be completely cool about it. I don't think we know who that guy really is."

"That's for damn sure."

Dakota goes back to working on her computer and Tinley's eyes trail Marek as he walks back to his desk. The situation is giving her whiplash, but she can't help herself from seeing him in a new light. Maybe he isn't such a bad guy after all.

ELEVEN

*U*ntil she started working at the call center, lunch wasn't that big of a deal to Tinley. Some days she would actually forget to eat and not even notice, but now that she works in a pretty sucky job, she starts counting down the seconds until lunchtime as soon as she steps foot on the floor. That should probably tell her something about her current work situation, but she still sticks around. She and Dakota have different lunch times since they work different schedules, so typically she just holes up in the corner of the break room and scrolls through social media. She lifts up her sandwich to take a bite then is surprised to see there's a text message from an unknown number waiting for her on her phone.

Unknown: Is it completely dorky of
me to be texting you already?

Is this one of those *wrong number and a smoking hot guy on the other end* scenarios? Because Tinley could definitely get on board with that. He'd be a Scottish Highlander with abs for days and adorably curly ginger locks, not to mention his alpha male tendencies mixed in with the biggest heart and eyes only for her. She internally swoons just imagining her knight wrapped in a tartan kilt. Okay, maybe she has been watching slightly too much *Outlander*, but she would throw her body through the stones a thousand times if it meant she could end up with a guy like James Alexander Malcolm MacKenzie Fraser. She internally swoons just imagining it, but knowing her luck, it's totally not, and the person on the other end would be very disappointed by her plain Jane, slightly overweight appearance, especially the extra pounds she's carrying in her midsection thanks to the aforementioned cupcakes. She shoots off a text and the little piece of her heart still hoping for a fantasy dies a little.

Me: I'm sorry. I think you have the
wrong number.

This is the part where her mystery suitor never replies and she can go back to her regularly scheduled programming, also known as recipe hunting for the batch of cupcakes she's making for Tara's baby shower. It was bad enough when she was a bridezilla and needed everything just right, but Tinley figured for something as simple as a baby shower, she'd tone it down a notch. No such luck. She's already made fifteen different kinds of cakes, and don't even get her started on the different fillings and frostings she's made. This shower is turning out to be way over the top, and this is baby number two, so it's not even like this is Tara's first time having a baby.

Tinley continues scrolling through Pinterest looking for ideas for flavor combinations. She creates all the recipes she actually bakes herself, but sometimes you need to go outside of your own brain to get ideas, and Pinterest is always good for that.

> **Unknown:** I hope I don't have the wrong number. That would be incredibly awkward. Since we never exchanged names, did we have a date a couple of nights ago?

Holy shit. It's one of the guys from the speed dating thing. This could go horribly badly or so deliciously well. She pushed any thoughts of him actually reaching out to her to the back of her mind and never expected to hear from him again, which gets her thinking: is this the guy she actually wants to be talking to right now? Odds are good that this is the fourth date she had from Dating in the Dark, but it's possible that this could still be a wrong number. She decides to play coy with him and see what kind of reaction she gets.

> **Me:** Possibly. I had a few dates that night...care to narrow it down for me? ;)

> **Unknown:** I can tell you with absolute certainty that I don't have anger management issues, I'm not interested in any kinky orgies, and I'm definitely not an alien. I'm pretty positive on that last one, but you never know.

She cracks up laughing as she reads through his message. It's definitely the guy she wants to be hearing from, and even through texts, their chemistry is undeniable. Remembering where she's at, she looks up and finds the break room atypically empty. It might look weird for her to be suddenly breaking out in laughter or smiling like an idiot while looking so intently at her phone. She thinks about her response for a moment and then shoots one off.

> **Me:** Ahh, so you're Mystery Date Number Four. I was wondering if I would ever hear from you again.

She quickly saves his number in her contacts so his messages don't keep popping up as from "Unknown". Part of her wants to ask him what his name is, but the other part of her is enjoying the mystery of not knowing, like it adds another layer of possibility to whatever this is that's starting up between them.

Mystery Date: You could have reached out to me first.

Me: Can I be honest with you about something?

Mystery Date: I'd rather you be honest than tell me a lie.

She sighs heavily and puts her phone down on the table. She opens up her yogurt and contemplates her reply to him. She could be really honest and lay out all her cards, or she could chicken out again and make something up, but something inside her says to be honest. That's the whole point of this experiment, right? There are no judgments or biases involved, so why not be completely open with him? The worst thing that could happen is he decides her specific brand of crazy is too much for him and they stop talking, and the best-case scenario is she's finally honest with herself and her partner in a relationship and things only get better from here. She quickly types out a response and hits send before she has the chance to second-guess herself.

> **Me:** I chickened out and didn't take your number. I filled out the card and asked for your number so you'd be able to get mine if you asked for it, but I didn't actually wait to get yours.

> **Mystery Date:** Because?

> **Me:** I totally thought you brushed me off at the end of our date.

> **Mystery Date:** What made you think that?

> **Me:** I said it was nice meeting you and I hoped to see you again soon and you said, 'It was good meeting you too.'

> **Mystery Date:** So?

So? Is he serious right now? Tinley rolls her eyes at his lack of understanding. How can he not understand that what he said implied he wasn't interested? They couldn't see each other so she had no way of judging body language. The only thing she had going for her were the words coming out of his mouth and not once did he says that he wanted to see her again too.

> **Me**: So how was I supposed to know you would want to see me again?

> **Mystery Date**: Do you realize how ridiculous you sound right now?

> **Me**: So, you don't want to see me again?

A chuckle comes from the other side of the room and Tinley watches as Marek looks down at his phone. She hadn't realized she wasn't alone. It's a good thing she opted for texting her mystery date back rather than talking to him on the phone. It's always been one of her biggest pet peeves when people have long private conversations in a public setting. You don't need to be telling everyone around you your business.

Her phone lights up with another message, and she can't help but smile.

> **Mystery Date**: Woman, do you think I would still be texting you right now if I didn't want to see you again?

Oddly enough she gets a small bought of butterflies

in her stomach at his response. She's never liked the idea of a man calling her *woman*, but the whole alpha male vibe it gives off kind of turns her on. Who knew?

> **Me:** I see your point there. Can't blame a girl for asking. After all, we haven't actually seen each other face to face yet.

The time on the corner of her phone screen catches her eye. Has it been an hour already? She's been so busy texting away and nibbling at her lunch, she didn't realize how quickly the time was passing by, but it means they now have to end their conversation.

> **Me:** Sadly, our little conversation must come to a close. My lunch break is over and it's pretty frowned upon for me to be texting at my desk.

> **Mystery Date:** How frowned upon?

> **Me:** More like I'd be fired if anyone saw me with my phone out.

> **Mystery Date:** Well we don't want that. Until next time then.

She can't wipe the huge smile that covers her face as she locks her phone and throws away the trash from her lunch. There's something about this guy, and she can't wait to get to know him better. She wonders for a moment what he looks like. He has a sexy voice that tells her he has to be good-looking, but she just doesn't know if she's ready to see him face to face. What if when they do finally meet, he decides she doesn't live up to whatever picture he has in his mind? That kind of rejection isn't something she wants to go through right now.

"What has you so happy Tinley?"

She doesn't turn around, just continues walking toward her desk. "Nothing at all Marek. Nothing at all."

TWELVE

*T*inley hits play as Netflix interrupted her bingeing session for the second time since she sat down this evening. After work, she went straight to the grocery store and picked up a new bottle of wine and the fixings to make a batch of cupcakes. She's a mood eater through and through so even though she still has cupcakes at home she wanted something different. She broke the cardinal rule of baking and frosted a couple of them straight out of the oven creating an ooey gooey mess of deliciousness. Combine that with the delicious on her screen and her night has gotten much better. Although, she can't help but wonder if it's weird that the two guys she's currently lusting after are drastically different in age?

Rather than contemplate that further, she continues

watching the shenanigans play out in front of her on the screen. Who knew a dark and brooding murder mystery esque Archie comics TV show could be so addicting? Definitely not Tinley. She finishes off the last bite of cupcake she has waiting on her plate and sets it aside. Picking up her phone, she decides to see what her Mystery Date is up to this evening.

Me: Hypothetical question.

Mystery Date: Okay, shoot.

Me: If someone were to carry five very heavy bags of groceries from their car to their apartment. Then proceed to spend hours baking cupcakes. Does that and clicking the button to let Netflix know they haven't gotten their life together and are still watching while eating said cupcakes, count as exercise?

Me: Asking for a friend, of course. ;)

Tinley pouts into her wine glass as she finishes the last drop and looks longingly at the kitchen. She's perfectly comfortable in her spot on the couch and she'd hate to have to ruin it by getting up. She found the best combination of pillow to blanket ratio and her toes are currently nice in toasty underneath her knitted throw. Although, she does wonder if she can still call it knitted since she bought it at Target this way. It was definitely mass produced on a machine.

Mystery Date: That depends.

Me: On?

Mystery Date: What kind of cupcakes are we talking about here?

Me: Does that really make a difference?

Mystery Date: Absolutely. The entire basis of your question relies heavily on that answer. If we're talking homemade red velvet with an insanely good cream cheese frosting that was mixed by hand, then *your friend* absolutely got in a workout. But if we're talking a box of cake mix and a tub of frosting. Then no way.

Me: Sacrilege. I would never bring that junk into my house.

Me: I mean. My friend. She makes everything from scratch when it comes to baking.

Mystery Date: Right. Your friend.

Me: Okay fine. It was me. That's what happens when you decide to have that second glass of wine I guess.

Mystery Date: Cupcakes and wine. Where was my invite?

Me: I don't think my living room could handle any more men tonight.

Mystery Date: Sounds kinky.

Me: If me simultaneously lusting over Cole Sprouse and Luke Perry counts as kinky, then so be it.

Mystery Date: Um. What?

> **Me:** I'm currently sucked into a *Riverdale* binge-fest on Netflix. I've had to click the button twice now to let Netflix know that my life is pathetic, and I have not moved from my spot on the couch.

She sends off that text and realizes she hasn't even been watching the TV since she picked up her phone. The entire cast could have died right in front of her and she wouldn't have even realized it.

> **Me:** I really need to stop drinking and texting. Because you know how lame I really am.

> **Mystery Date:** I don't think you're lame or pathetic. Sounds to me like you're enjoying yourself and that's all that really matters.

Tinley can't help but smile at his response. Not her fake customer service smile but a full-blown real one. It covers her entire face and her cheeks heat up in response. Part of that is due to the two glasses of wine she consumed but the rest is all for

Me: I have zero words. That was probably the sweetest thing any guy has ever said to me.

Mystery Date: Obviously you've been talking to the wrong guys then.

"What has you grinning like an idiot?"

The phone slips from her fingers and she jumps as Dakota comes up behind her. It doesn't seem like she actually saw what was on her phone screen, so Tinley just waves her hand and says, "Oh it was just some video I saw on social media. I thought it was funny."

She walks toward the kitchen while yelling over her shoulder, "Oh, was one of the ones with that toddler girl who talks like she's an adult?"

Tinley racks her brain for whatever her best friend is talking about but comes up with nothing. Meanwhile, her phone vibrates underneath her, and she tries to ignore it. Dakota walks back in with a cheese string, the bottle of wine, and a glass and takes a seat on the couch. Tinley is itching to grab her cell but replies to Dakota's question instead. "No, I don't think I've watched any of those."

Dakota pours herself a glass and refills Tinley's at the same time. Both of their attention gravitates toward the TV and Dakota claps her hand causing Tinley to jump on the couch yet again. "I bet it was one of those reaction videos, right?"

Her phone vibrates again in her lap and she wants nothing more than to pick it up and read the messages that he's sent her. All of her focus is fixated on that phone and she shakes her head realizing that Dakota asked her a question.

"Um, what?"

"The funny video you were talking about earlier."

Funny video? What funny video? She has no idea what her best friend is talking about she nods and says, "Oh sure. Something like that."

Dakota raises an eyebrow in question but Tinley ignores it standing up from the couch with her phone and glass of wine in her hand. "Sorry, I'm getting tired. Must be all the wine and sugar crash from the cupcakes. I'm going to head to bed."

"Ooookay," Dakota says stretching out the "o," in her response.

Without a backward glance, Tinley hurries down the hallway toward her room to read his responses. With the door shut tightly behind her, she places her glass of wine down on her dresser and opens up her text messages.

Mystery Date: Or people? I probably shouldn't assume you're only into dudes.

Mystery Date: Shit. Did I piss you off?

She chuckles to herself as she types out a response.

Me: Sorry, my roommate came into the room and distracted me for a minute. I'm very much into guys. I've never kissed a girl before, but I don't think I'd like it. ;)

Me: Like that Katy Perry reference?

Me: Shit. Maybe I should put the glass of wine down and my phone down. I'm starting to get rambly with my messages.

Mystery Date: Don't mind me. You're entertaining as hell right now.

Me: I think I'm going to cut myself off and head to bed before I say anything stupid to you.

Mystery Date: Haha! Sweet dreams babe. I hope you feel okay in the morning.

Even though they've only had the one date, Tinley melts a little at the term of endearment. She's never had someone call her by a pet name before, then again, they still don't actually know each other's names. Although the added mystery does make this whole thing more fun. She dumps the remainder of her glass of wine in the sink and climbs into bed. She can't wipe the smile off her face as she gets cozy and slips off to dreamland.

THIRTEEN

*T*inley always finds herself debating ridiculous topics when she's taking a shower. For instance, this morning while she was putting shampoo in her hair, she wondered if people really spit in food at restaurants. She's never personally had it happen to her as far as she knows, but she's seen it on TV enough times to wonder if it actually happens. Of course, that led her down a tangent and she contemplated the idea that if people are willing to spit in food at restaurants, where is the line drawn and what else do they do to food? When she got to thinking about some dude jizzing in mayonnaise, she gagged and had to stop that line of thought altogether, especially since she was running conditioner through her hair at the time.

This morning's thought process lengthened her

shower more than usual so she had to rush to finish getting ready and out the door. It wasn't until she pulled into the parking lot at work fifteen minutes later that she realized she was in fact early for work today. So, of course, she pulled out her cell phone and was pleasantly surprised to see a message waiting for her.

Mystery Date: Good morning.

Me: Good morning to you too. I had a ridiculous morning and it was nice to see your message waiting for me.

Mystery Date: Yeah, what happened?

Me: Nothing too eventful. I just got lost in thought while I was in the shower and thought I was going to be late for work. Turns out I'm here ten minutes early.

Mystery Date: In the shower, huh? Were they naughty thoughts?

Her cheeks redden as she thinks of him thinking about her in the shower. That's not even how she meant for it to come across, but she sees exactly why he would think so. She could continue on down that line of thinking and see where the conversation leads, or she could tell him the truth. Seeing as she's about ready to go in for an eight-hour shift at work, now is not the ideal time to get all hot and bothered.

> **Me:** Wouldn't that be exciting? No, I actually got some shampoo in my mouth and spit it out. It got me thinking about whether or not people actually spit in food at restaurants or if that's just something they make up on TV, and then I got lost on a tangent of what else people put in food for shitty customers.

She sends the long text message and starts gathering up her stuff for the day. The frigid morning air hits her face and she quickens her pace as she heads toward the front of the building. She scans her badge to get in and is instantly hit with a wave of heat as it floats outside. She glances down at her phone and takes a seat in one of the lobby chairs to finish off her conversation.

> **Mystery Date:** Definitely not just something made up for TV.

> **Me:** Oh? Do you know this from personal experience? Or do you

> have a friend in the restaurant
> industry?
>
> **Mystery Date:** Both actually. I know
> someone in the industry and I
> worked as a waiter while I was
> in college. Trust me, if you ever
> want to eat at a restaurant
> again, you don't want to know
> what some people have put in food
> before.
>
> **Me:** I'll take your word for it. That
> does not sound like something I
> want to know.

Her bags go onto her shoulder as she uses her badge yet again to get onto the calling floor. She's walking toward her desk when her phone dings with a notification. She glances down but ignores is at she makes her way over to her desk. A voice comes from behind her and she jumps at the booming sound.

"Tinley, are you seriously texting someone right now? Do you not know that our ability to run credit cards for our customers could be completely compromised if someone saw your cell phone out? What are you thinking right now?"

"Marek, calm down. It's just in my hand, and it's not like I'm even at my desk right now."

"No, you're not at your desk, but the moment you stepped foot on the sales floor, your phone should have been out of sight. C'mon, you've worked here long enough to know this. I shouldn't have to explain it to you."

Tinley slides her phone into her hoodie pocket and raises her hands. "All gone. No worries."

"I don't feel like you're taking this seriously right now. Does PCI compliance mean anything to you?"

"You're taking this way too far. It's not like I was anywhere near a computer. We're fine. Just let me get back to work."

He continues talking to her, but she pretends to not hear him as she walks over to her desk. *Geez.* Dakota tells her on a daily basis that she needs to get laid, but it seems like the person who is really dealing with that issue is Marek. He at least needs to get that stick up his ass pulled out. It's like he's dead set on making her day worse than it has to be.

As soon as Tinley's break comes up, she's up and out of her seat as quickly as possible. Normally she lingers a bit to catch a call coming in, but she doesn't even care about that anymore. She's mostly eager to read the text message that's waiting on her phone from this morning. It's been burning a hole in her hoodie pocket for the past two hours, and now she can finally catch a glimpse of it.

> **Mystery Date:** See, I knew you were smart.

The simple text makes her smile. He was totally complimenting himself on the fact that she agreed with what he had to say, but he complimented her at the same time too. It's so completely high school for her to be getting this excited about it, but she can't help herself. Out of the corner of her eye, she watches as Marek heads outside. She absolutely hates that they have identical work schedules. Every single day they work at the exact same time and have their breaks and lunches together. It's totally annoying, but she doesn't have a legitimate reason to ask for her schedule to be changed. Plus, she's afraid if she were to ask for a schedule change, they'd move her to the swing shift, and that's the last thing she wants. She actually likes her schedule, minus this annoyance, so she puts up with it.

> **Me:** How many times can you imagine stabbing needles through your boss's head before it becomes excessive?

> **Mystery Date:** Depends. On a scale

```
from one to uber douche, where
does he/she land?
```

She cracks up laughing at that one. She's never met someone else, besides Dakota, who likes to mix it up and not just use douchebag all the time as an insult. In fact, when they're really bored they'll come up with different variations. They've been known to curl up on the couch with a bottle of wine and Urban Dictionary a time or two.

Me: We'll definitely put him into the doucheasaurus rex category.

Mystery Date: That's a new one for me. I'm going to assume that's bad and say as many times as you need to in order to help get you through the day.

Me: I like your thinking. What about you? Do you have asshole bosses you have to put up with?

Mystery Date: Of course, who doesn't? But I'm in that awkward position of having bosses and being a boss at the time same.

Me: Well I hope you at least like your job. I could never be management at the place where I work—too much politics.

Mystery Date: You'll find that pretty much anywhere you work though.

Me: I wouldn't know, I haven't had many jobs.

Mystery Date: Are you that young? Or have you just stuck around at the same place for a long time?

Me: Fishing for my age, are we? How old are you?

Mystery Date: It would be nice to know how old you are. I at least know you're legal since you had to be twenty-one to do the speed dating, but other than that, it's a complete mystery to me. I'm 35.

She contemplates playing with him and seeing how far she can take this. She kind of enjoys the banter that they always have together, but playing coy about her age seems almost juvenile and pointless. Besides, since he's already thirty-five he probably doesn't want to be with a young girl that plays games. She needs to act more mature. More like her age.

Me: 29

Mystery Date: That is a relief. I don't think I could handle being with someone ten years younger than me. I'd like to date a grown-up.

Me: That's me, grown-up girl who's stayed too long at a job she hates. With that, I'll leave you for the time being. Back to work it is.

This time she instantly puts her phone back into her hoodie pocket. She'd rather not have a repeat of this morning if Marek catches her carrying her phone, but if Mystery Date sends another text right away, she doesn't want to wait two hours to find out what it says. That was just too much for her anxiety last time and made her morning stretch on for days. Maybe, if she's lucky, this time she'll get busy and time will fly by.

FOURTEEN

The last drop of wine slides down her throat and she hums in satisfaction. She picked out a new brand to try this time around and was not disappointed with the results. The fruit flavors were incredibly fresh and crisp with the perfect mix of sweet and dry. If there's one thing she can't stand is an overly dry glass of wine and anything too sweet makes her sick to stomach before she can even finish her first glass. She drops the glass off in the kitchen and pads her way down to her bedroom. She starts getting undressed for the evening when her phone dings with a new text message alert.

Surprisingly her day passed by incredibly fast. After her texting conversation with Mystery Date this morning, she kept it up and continued chatting with him on her lunch and afternoon break. He was super-fast to reply both times and she couldn't hide her giddiness. She has no idea what he does for work, but obviously, his work place is more flexible when it comes to using his phone. Now that she thinks about it, they haven't really discussed what either one of them do for work. Not that she's too eager to share the fact that she's spent most of her twenties working at a call center and she hasn't progressed at all in her career.

> **Mystery Date:** As much as I enjoy texting back and forth with you, don't you think we should go on that second date?

The phone slips from her fingers and clatters on the floor below. A second date? She knew it was coming eventually, but it feels soon—too soon. What if she gets to wherever they decide to go and he realizes how much of a mistake he made? That the girl standing in front of him is not what he had in mind at all?

> **Me:** A second date?

> **Mystery Date:** Even though we couldn't see each other, we technically already had the first date. What if you've been chatting with me this entire time and I'm a hideous beast? ;)

The winking face at the end of his text indicates that he meant it as a joke, but in reality, this is what she's afraid of—not that he will be ugly, but that he won't be okay with the way she looks. It's not like she's going to be winning any beauty pageants any time soon.

> **Me:** I highly doubt you're a hideous beast, and besides, I'm not shallow. I wouldn't suddenly stop talking to you based on your looks. Would you do that to me?

She does secretly hope he is as attractive on the outside as he is on the inside.

> **Mystery Date:** Not possible. I already know you're gorgeous.

> **Me:** How can you tell? You've never seen me before.

> **Mystery Date:** Because there's more to a person than how they look on the outside. So far I like everything about you, so I don't foresee that changing just because we meet face to face.

She glances up at the mirror in front of her. She's

never referred to herself as ugly before, but gorgeous is definitely not the word to describe her either. She's been called plain Jane, average, and up until this point in her life, she's been accustomed to it. That's just who she is and she's okay with it, but now Mystery Date has her questioning everything. What if she's not good enough for him because she's just average? He says physical appearances don't matter, but everyone says that. That's the nice thing to say until the true colors come out, and they always do.

> **Mystery Date:** Good, we're on the same page then.

> **Mystery Date:** Meet me at Big House Bookstore on Friday at eight.

Big House Bookstore? She's never even heard of that place before. She sends off a quick reply that she'll be there and does an internet search to find the address. If anything, Friday will bring new adventures, and potentially more than that. She hasn't been this excited in a long time, and now she's counting down the minutes until the big night.

The aroma of lavender and chamomile surrounds Tinley as she sinks deeper and deeper into her bathtub. She decided to light every calming candle she owns and fill her bathtub with lavender bubble bath. Either she'll be incredibly calm or she'll fall asleep. Not that the latter would be the worst-case scenario at this point. She definitely needs to chill the fuck out.

She can't afford to go on vacations, so every once in a while, she'll use her vacation time to take a Friday off and give herself a three-day weekend. It just so happens that she had already requested today off from work, and she hasn't been able to decide if that was a good thing or a bad thing. Sure, she was able to sleep in, but since waking up, her nerves have gotten the better of her, hence the supposedly soothing bathtub. No matter what she does to try to calm herself down, she can't help but go into freak-out mode thinking about her date tonight. She keeps running all the what-ifs through her mind, and they're making her anxiety skyrocket.

She thought about doing a little drinking, but she definitely doesn't want to show up completely smashed, and even her normal therapy of baking cupcakes isn't working. At least a dozen times, she's picked up her phone to send a text canceling the date, but every time, she talks herself out of it. Even though the thought of putting herself out there like this is terrifying, she'd always wonder *what if*, and that is the biggest what-if of them all.

She doesn't want to have regrets about this life and

the things she could have done. She wants to look back and know with absolute certainty that she did everything she was supposed to and then some. Sitting on the sidelines watching her own life pass her by isn't something she wants to keep doing. That's really what this whole thing was about in the first place. Tara and Dakota weren't pushing her to do this so she would have a man in her life, although that was a plus; it was to get her to finally do something outside her comfort zone, to finally force her to live a little, and she has no desire to let either one of them—or herself—down.

She slides her fingers down her leg, loving the feeling of them being freshly shaved. She has no idea how tonight is going to go, but she figured to err on the side of optimism and be prepared just in case. Before starting her bath, she took a shower and shaved. Everything. It took a good forty-five minutes, but it was definitely worth it and if tonight goes well she'll be happy that she prepared. It's been a long time since the last time she had sex, so she's a little nervous just thinking about the mechanics of it all, but if their chemistry stays the same once they're face to face, they don't have anything to worry about. At least that's what she hopes.

FIFTEEN

*I*t's just a date. No big deal.

She has repeated that mantra no less than fifty times since she pulled her car into the bookstore's parking lot, not to mention the number of times she tried tricking herself into believing it as she was getting ready for the night. Still, no matter how many times she tells herself this, it doesn't change the fact that it's not true. No part of this is *no big deal*. In fact, it's a really huge deal. She can't remember the last time she went on a date with someone, let alone someone she's been talking to but hasn't ever seen with her own eyes. Fortunately, there's no risk of catfishing here since they've already met in person.

She didn't question her date's location choice when he offered it up, but now that she's here, it does seem like an odd venue. Then again, maybe he's a major bookworm and wants to know what kinds of books she reads, like a test or something. She walks inside and is immediately hit with that scent of old books. She's not huge on reading, but she can't deny the appeal of the musty smell. The room is filled with bookshelf upon bookshelf, and there are so many books they're pretty much everywhere. The shelves are filled to the brim and even the floor in front of each shelf has stacks lined up. If she were a bigger reader she could imagine being in heaven in a place like this. She walks around and sees another room in the corner hidden by a curtain. She's way too intrigued to pass that by and heads straight toward it.

Though the curtain, she's met with a smaller room and even more bookshelves. There are more stacks of books on the floor back here as well. There are hundreds of them in this small space, and it looks more like a storage room than an actual part of the store. She starts to turn around when movement catches her attention out of the corner of her eye. There's a guy standing near one of the shelves, and he's looking right at her. "What's the password?"

Tinley looks behind her and back to the man standing in front of her. What is this guy talking about? A password? Is she in the wrong place? She can feel heat travel up her neck as she mumbles out, "Password? I'm supposed to be meeting a date here."

The guy tips his fedora and pulls on his suspenders. "You mean to tell me your date didn't tell you about this place?"

"What place is that exactly? He told me we were going to a bookstore. Well, actually he just gave me the name of this place and told me to meet him here, I had to look it up online to find out where it was even located. I don't know what you're talking about."

"You're in for a treat then." Without another word, he walks over to the shelf and pulls down on one of the books. The shelf swings wide open and the low, sultry sound of jazz music flows from within. The lights are dimmed down low, so Tinley isn't quite sure what's she getting herself into. The guy standing at the door leans over before she steps in and whispers in her ear, "Enjoy your evening. If anyone asks, the password is Capone."

She turns back around and looks at him questioningly. "As in Al Capone? That's weird."

"You'll see," he adds with a wink before turning back around.

Too intrigued to question him any further, she steps fully into the room as the door shuts tightly behind her with a click. A small part of her is scared of the unknown, but a larger part of her is too excited by all the mystery piling onto this evening. Even if it's a bust with the guy she's supposed to be meeting, this right here will make the outing worthwhile. She studies her surroundings and finds herself in a long cold stone hallway. The walls are lined with electric candelabras and the music floats into the hallway from speakers overhead.

The light is brighter at the end of the hall and with

nowhere else to turn to, she heads in that direction. Her heels click-clack against the cobblestone floors beneath her, and she can't help but feel transported to 1920s Chicago when Prohibition was in full swing and speakeasies were rampant. Assuming this room was set up to mimic that style, she quickens her pace in excitement to get to the end of the passageway and enter the room.

There's so much going on, and she has no idea where to look at first, but then her eyes zero directly in on the bar. The wall behind it is lined all the way to the ceiling with different liquor bottles. There have to be hundreds of them, if not a thousand, and that's exactly where she heads. If her date isn't here yet, she needs just a little something to help her relax for when he does arrive. She pulls out one of the empty bar stools and takes a seat. It's still pretty early and there aren't many customers in the bar, so the bartender comes right over to her. He's cute with a boy-next-door kind of vibe, and she would totally flirt with him if she weren't meeting a date here—or maybe he is her date? It's possible, but she quickly shakes that thought from her mind.

"What can I get you to drink?"

She racks her brain, unsure of what to order. She is normally just a wine drinker, but she feels like that wouldn't be appropriate in a place like this. There's an ambiance in here and with the whole speakeasy thing, she wants to stick to that. That definitely doesn't make her decision on what to get easier though. She remembers something about bathtub gin being a thing back then...or something like that...so she pretends to be fancy and says, "I'm not really sure. What would you suggest with gin in it?"

His mouth drops open and he starts laughing, a full-blown belly laugh. "You're kidding, right?"

She grimaces slightly. Obviously, that was the wrong answer. "Um, how about a drink menu?"

He continues laughing, nods his head, and grabs a monstrosity from the counter behind him. He drops it in front of her, and she's pretty sure the thing is thicker than The Cheesecake Factory's menu. How is that even possible?

The front reads, *Fitzgerald's, home of over four hundred varieties of gin*. Well, now she feels like an idiot. No wonder he was laughing his ass off at her inquiry. If she'd known the password to get in here, she sure as hell would have known about the drink menu. She runs her finger down the menu and stops on something called "The Gatsby" then tells the bartender to make her that. She read *The Great Gatsby* in high school and assumes the drink is named after the famous book, and the combination of gin, cherry liqueur, and orange bitters sounds like it could be pretty tasty.

While he's making her drink, she continues looking through the menu. She can't get over how extensive it is. Who knew there were so many different ways to make a gin cocktail? When she reaches the end of the menu, she can't help but laugh at the limited selection of beer and wine, only four different varieties of each. Guess they'd much rather serve a different kind of crowd here.

As the bartender places the drink on the bar in front of her, she starts to offer her thanks, but the words get caught in her throat. Over his shoulder, in the mirror behind the bar, she spots Marek Outlaw walking in. *Shit.* How can she have a romantic get-together with her mystery date while her boss is in the room? Talk about awkward. Maybe he won't spot her and she can slip out and send her date somewhere else. She doesn't like spending all day with the guy at work; no way she's going to let him have a front row seat to her date.

Of course, luck is never on her side. As she continues staring at him in the mirror, he looks up and his eyes meet hers. She quickly looks back down to the bar, hoping with everything inside of her that he didn't see her, or that he'll at least pretend like he didn't see her and they can just act like they don't know each other.

"Tinley Scott, funny running into you here. This doesn't really seem like your kind of place."

It's on the tip of her tongue to tell him she's actually never been here before and that she's meeting someone, but something about the way he said it has her all riled up and pissed off. "Oh, because you know me so well that you know what kind of places I go to?"

He motions for the bartender and takes a seat on the stool next to her. She wants to tell him to get up and walk away, but she's suddenly fascinated by the concoction the bartender is making in front of them. She doesn't recall

Marek actually ordering a drink, but maybe she just wasn't paying enough attention. Starting off with a shot glass the bartender adds a mixture of Bailey's and Jameson to the small container. He then reaches for a pint glass and pours Guinness in straight from the tap. It isn't until he drops the shot glass into the beer and Marek immediately proceeds to down the whole thing that she realizes what just happened.

"What the hell kind of drink was that?"

Marek chuckles and licks off the bit of foam from the top of his lip. Fuck why was that so damn sexy? He leans down close to her and her heart rate speeds up as his lips get so close to hers they're almost touching. "That would be what you'd call an Irish Car Bomb."

She can feel his breath on her lips, and if she stuck her tongue out just slightly, she'd be touching his. Before she can get her wits about her, he continues talking. "I don't know anything about the places where you go. I just meant I've been here a time or two and have never seen you here."

She looks up into the mirror and sees he has the smuggest grin on his face. "For your information, this is my first time coming here, though I don't really need to explain myself to you. Now, can you please leave? I'm meeting a date and would rather not have you scare him away."

"Is that so?"

She nods. "It is. In fact, I'll text him right now. He's probably already here." She pulls out her phone and opens the conversation she was having with Mystery Date. Typing up a quick message, she sends it off to him and waits.

> **Me:** Hey I'm here. I'm sitting at the bar and looking extra fabulous tonight. I'm wearing a black off-the-shoulder top and I've got cherry red lipstick on my lips.

She adds a kissing emoji to the end and then contemplates whether or not that was a good idea. She shrugs, takes a large sip of her cocktail, and decides it was the best idea...though that might be the alcohol talking.

She hears a ding, and Marek digs into the front pocket of his jeans then pulls his phone out. He glances down at the screen then up at Tinley, and his eyes go wide. She wants to ask him what's going on, but instead, he flips his phone around and shows her the message he just got.

> **Mystery Babe:** Hey I'm here. I'm sitting at the bar and looking extra fabulous tonight. I'm wearing a black off-the-shoulder top and I've got cherry red lipstick on my lips.

No. No. No. This cannot be happening. The gorgeous guy she's been talking to and completely connecting with cannot be the jerk she works with. There's no way the universe would be as cruel as that. She looks up at his face and sees the remorse written all over it. She quickly stands up from her bar stool, and her legs start to buckle. He gets up to help her, but she puts her hand in the air to stop him. "I'm sorry, this is a mistake." She motions between the two of them. "Whatever this is, it can't happen. I'm sorry."

Then she grabs her purse and flees the room without a backward glance.

SIXTEEN

*M*arek Outlaw? What are the odds that the one person who pisses her off the most and is her boss was her mystery dream date? This is just her luck, though it's not actually her fault—it's Dakota and Tara's fault. They pushed her into this whole speed-dating-in-the-dark thing. She didn't want to have anything to do with it, and this is what she has to show for it.

So annoying.

Dammit, she feels incredibly stupid for not realizing it was him in the first place. She spends so much time thinking about how incredibly sexy his voice would sound during sex and yet she was so discombobulated during their speed date the thought never crossed her mind. And, why would it? Marek is a fucking girl's wet dream come to life, why the hell was he even there in the first place. Women have to be throwing their panties at him on a regular basis. People who look like him, don't need help in the dating department that's for sure.

She scoops another cup of flour into the bowl as she works on a new cupcake recipe. As annoying as it sounds, Marek's drink last night gave her inspiration: Guinness and dark chocolate cupcakes with a caramel whiskey buttercream frosting. Her mouth starts watering just thinking about it. She even came up with a cute name for them: Irish Cake Bombs.

She mindlessly hums along to the song on the radio as she quickly mixes the dry ingredients together. Her bangs fall into her eyes, and she tucks the loose strands behind her ear without missing a beat. She dances along to the song as the singer preaches about wanting to "Feel Good," getting her body into a rhythm with each sway and mix of the spoon. She gets so lost in what she's doing that she almost misses it when her phone vibrates across the counter as a new text message comes in. She wipes her flour-covered hand across the bottom of her shirt and picks it up. Surprisingly, a text from Marek is waiting on her screen, and she thinks maybe she should change his name in her contacts. On second thought, maybe she should just delete his number from her phone. That's probably the smarter plan.

Mystery Date: Tinley, look, last
night didn't go the way either
one of us had planned, but I
think we were too hasty in our
decision.

Her heart rate picks up a notch. Too hasty? What does he mean by that? He couldn't mean he actually wants to give this a try, could he? She quickly combines all the wet and dry ingredients together. While mixing the cupcake batter with one hand, she sends another text with the other.

Me: Explain further.

Her anxiety skyrockets as the familiar three dots pop up, alerting her to the fact that he's typing a response. Part of her knows this is a bad idea, and she can't possibly see how it could go well. As it is, they constantly argue at work, and that's not very stable ground to start a relationship on. On the other hand, that's how they are at work. Most couples don't work together because they just can't, and between the first date and their texting conversations, being with Marek seems right, like they fit together and he could be the one. How do you deny yourself the person who could possibly be your soul mate? The answer is, you don't. If you only get one perfect person for you in this life, you don't let anything stand in the way of finding that person.

Mystery Date: We have a connection, one I can't even describe, but I think we should explore it further. We shouldn't let something as small as me being your boss prevent us from seeing where this goes.

Me: What about the fact that it's against company policy?

Mystery Date: As far as I'm concerned, it isn't anyone else's business besides our own. If whatever this is between us becomes serious, we'll deal with it then. Until then, we don't even know what it is, so there's no reason to tell anyone anything.

Me: Marek Outlaw, are you saying you want me to be your dirty little secret?

She again contemplates leaving his name as Mystery Date in her phone but then types his name instead. Something about having his real name pop up on the screen any time a text or phone call comes through feels even more deliciously deceptive, like they could get caught at any moment, and the idea of that thrills her to no end.

Tinley giggles to herself as she puts her phone down and continues mixing the batter. She knew what he meant when he sent that text, but she can't help but mess with him a little bit. She releases a small squeal when her phone suddenly starts ringing, and Marek's name pops up on the screen. It's not something she expected at all. This situation calls for a little extra help, and fortunately, she's got just the thing. She cracks open the bottle of Jameson sitting in front of her and takes a couple of heavy swigs, which instantly go straight to her head. *Ugh*. She's such a lightweight.

She picks up her phone and accepts the call before she questions her own sanity. "H-Hello?"

"I want you to get one thing straight: I never said I wanted to keep you a secret. I only said we should wait and see where things go before we add in the politics from work. I'm not the kind of dick who would hide a relationship, so get that through your head right now. There's no point in stirring up shit at work if this thing crashes and burns."

Oh, she can't just leave that comment be. She chugs another shot of the whiskey down, and this time the intensity is lessened. If anything, she's just starting to feel warm and good...so good. "So now we're going to crash and burn? Gee Marek, I'm not sure I want to start something up with you if you're already planning out how it's going to end."

"Fuck, are you drunk right now?"

How can he tell? She's only had a few sips, not enough to actually do enough damage...*right?* Her head swims slightly as she looks down at the bottle in front of her. *When did that happen?* A third of the bottle seems to be missing, and she hasn't even started making the frosting yet. *Oops.* Maybe she had a little bit more than she thought. She giggles again and steadies herself against the counter. "I may have enjoyed a bit of the whiskey I'm using to make cupcakes."

"Whiskey cupcakes? That's a thing?"

She giggles and realizes she might just be a little drunk after all. "No silly, I'm putting beer in the cupcakes. The whiskey is for the frosting. I'm making Irish Cake Bombs. Let's just say I had a little inspiration."

There's a long pause at the other end, and she almost asks if he's still there, but then his voice comes over the line. "So you've been thinking about me?"

Shit. She didn't mean to let him know that.

"That's pretty sexy. I've been thinking about you too."

That statement is enough to sober her up a bit. She stands up straighter and completely forgets about the cupcake fixings in front of her. Her voice cracks a little as she responds, "You have?"

"Mhmm."

Something about the way his voice hums through the phone gets her all hot and bothered, and thoughts like that make her wonder what else he can do with that mouth of his, what the vibrations would feel like against her body. She collapses against the counter behind her and places her hand over her rapidly beating heart.

"What else have you been thinking about?" she asks boldly as she starts playing with the neckline of her shirt.

"Is that what we're doing now?"

She runs her hand down her torso, lightly grazing her nipple, and continues down, teasing the hemline of her top. "Maybe? Is that what you want to do right now?"

His breathing comes out a little heavier when he says, "I'd rather our first time having sex be in person, but seeing as I'm currently trapped at home I'd settle for a little phone sex."

The thrill travels through her body as she teases the hemline of her yoga pants. She runs her hand down the front of the outside and throws her head back and lets out a throaty moan as her fingers graze over her clit.

"Fuck that was sexy. Please tell me you're touching yourself right now."

Bringing her hand back up she slips her hand underneath her waistband and on a sigh she replies, "Mhmm."

She hears his zipper slide down, and her entire body lights up on fire. "Tell me what you're doing to yourself right now Tinley. I want to hear that sexy mouth say naughty things." He groans from his end, and she can hear the friction of his hand sliding up and down himself.

She pushes her hand inside of her panties and her finger dances along her nub. She almost screams out as intensity of pleasure shoots through her body. She picks up her speed racing toward a release that she knows won't take her long at all. As she continues pleasuring herself she pants out, "I—"

"Hey, do you have a bottle of wine open in here? I could really use a drink right now."

Shit. Without even thinking about it, she quickly rips her phone away from her ear and hits *end.* She tosses it onto the counter and reaches into the cupboard behind her for a glass. Dakota comes walking into the kitchen as Tinley is downing a glass of cold water.

"Are you okay, you look a little flushed and are you drinking whiskey? Since when do we have the hard stuff?"

Tinley laughs, but it comes out forced. She takes another gulp of water. "I was browsing Pinterest and found a recipe I wanted to recreate, sort of. Irish Cake Bomb cupcakes."

"Ooh sounds good." Dakota fills a glass with wine and starts heading out of the kitchen, but then she turns around. "You'll have to let me know when they're done."

Tinley nods and heaves a sigh of relief when her roommate is out of sight. Her phone comes back into view and she quickly sends off a text to Marek. She doesn't anticipate being able to salvage her impromptu phone sex date, but she needs to at least send an explanation text as to why she suddenly hung up the phone.

> **Me:** Sorry. Dakota came home and I panicked.

> **Marek:** Don't start something if you can't finish it Tinley. I should punish you for leaving me with a case of blue balls.

She waves her hand in front of her face and finishes off her glass of water. Why does the sound of that turn her on so bad? She's never been into the whole BDSM thing and she couldn't finish the popular book that everyone else at work was raving about, but she could get on board with a little naked spanking from Marek. Maybe she has a little kink in her after all?

> **Marek:** Meet me for drinks Monday night after work.

> **Me:** Okay.

Is she really going to do this? Is she going to date Marek Outlaw? It sounds like a horrible idea when she puts it like that, and the one person she wants to talk it over with is someone she can't tell about it. Even if they didn't work together, Dakota despises Marek and has always said as much, but she can't let her best friend's feelings affect her relationships, can she? The thought runs through her mind over and over as she abandons her cupcakes to jump in the shower. She is thoroughly hot and bothered and she has way too much on her mind to even consider trying to finish herself off. No, instead a nice long cold shower is just what she needs. And maybe it'll help with giving her a little more clarity on the situation. She hopes.

SEVENTEEN

$\int$he's a chicken, one giant bocking chicken. She called in sick to work this morning so she wouldn't have to see Marek. Even after her cold shower last night and running every possibility through her head, she wasn't much clearer on things when she woke up this morning. What would she even say to him? She couldn't handle the uncertainty of what they're going to talk about tonight, and she knows this is a bad idea. No good could actually come of them starting something up together, but she can't resist the urge to try. Getting to know Marek outside of work with no biases in place has been pretty surreal. He's funny and conversation between them flows easily, not to mention she's always been attracted to him— who wouldn't be? With that thick dark hair, piercing eyes, and a body she wants wrapped around her own, he's pretty irresistible.

He's already sitting there waiting for her when she arrives at the bar. She didn't know how to dress tonight and pretty much everything from her closet is on her bed or bedroom floor. When nothing in her own closet satisfied her, she ended up at the mall going through every single store until she landed on a simple black fit-and-flare dress with cap sleeves and a red plaid skirt. Splurging, she also bought a brand-new pair of black leather moto booties to match. If anything, she's feeling cute and confident going into this date, which reminds her of what Tara was telling her about the speed-dating date. Unfortunately, that time her sister was trying to get her to wear something completely outside of her comfort zone.

The moment his eyes meet hers as she approaches the table, her entire body feels like it could burst into flames with the amount of heat he's putting off. He scans every inch of her body then mouths, "Fuck me," and her desire intensifies. He stands up from the table and pulls her chair out for her then pushes it in as she takes a seat. As he pushes her in, he leans down much farther than necessary, and his mouth glides past her ear.

Her mouth is suddenly beyond dry, and she takes a sip of the water in front of her. She needs to get her head on straight, and that does not include him distracting her. Even though he's got his damn sleeves rolled up again showing off those delicious forearms. She licks her lips. Damn. She shakes her head and takes another giant gulp of water.

After allowing herself a moment of clarity she remembers one tiny detail and asks her question. "Won't your girlfriend be upset that you're on a date with me right now?"

He tilts his head to the side and sets his own drink back down on the table. A glass of whiskey by the looks of it, he definitely knows what he likes and sticks to it. He mulls what she says over for a moment and shrugs. "I give up. My girlfriend?"

"The gorgeous leggy brunette I saw you with at the coffee shop when I was with my sister. The day of our first date."

The moment the lightbulb goes off, his response is the last thing she expects. He leans his head back and lets out a ridiculously loud laugh. Allowing him his moment of hysteria, she motions for the waitress to come over and orders a glass of wine.

As she's walking away from the table, she looks over at Marek and asks, "Is he okay?"

Tinley shrugs and Marek's hysterics starts slowing down. He waves off the waitress and turns to Tinley. "I'm good. That was a funny joke. Hilarious."

"You want to clarify? What did I say that was just so funny?"

He picks up his glass draining the remaining contents as the waitress sets Tinley's glass of on wine on the table. The waitress glances at Marek's empty drink glass, opens her mouth, and then shakes her head and starts to walk away. Before she can make it very far, he turns around and says, "I'll take another."

She nods and heads straight toward the bar. While the waitress is gone, Tinley takes a heavy swig from her glass trying to avoid conversation at all costs. There's a basket of bread in the middle of the table and she makes quick work of stuffing her face. Moments later she's back with his drink and Marek swirls the glass in his hand.

Avoidance has not always been her strong suit, and her impatience wins out. Not wanting to beat around the bush, she comes right out with her question. "Are we really doing this? Exploring this further?"

He takes a drink from his small tumbler of brown liquid and contemplates her words. She's dying from agony when he finally offers up an answer. "I don't see why we wouldn't. If we didn't know each other and didn't work together, there would be no question. We would absolutely continue this, so why complicate things with shit that doesn't matter?"

She can think of a million different reasons why this is a bad idea, and she starts out with the most obvious one. "What about work?"

He places his drink on the table and calmly says, "Fuck work."

His bluntness shocks her and turns her on all at the same time. If he's not worried about the consequences at work, why should she be? Especially when he has more to lose than she does.

She leans forward for another piece of bread and his focus travels down her neckline and straight to her cleavage. The heat in his eyes intensifies, and she pats herself on the back for grabbing this dress. She's always told herself that she needs to lose the extra fifty pounds she's carrying around, but the one major upside is her ample breast size and the sweetheart neckline on this dress only reinforces what she has on top. With every graze of his eyes across her body, she feels sexier and bolder than she's ever felt before in her life.

Tinley polishes off the rest of her glass and stands up from the table. Marek stands at the same time. "I'm just going to the bathroom. I'll be right back."

He nods but looks uncertain as she turns to walk away. If she were going to skip out on him, she wouldn't lie about it, that's for sure. She has to see him every day at work, and ghosting him wouldn't be a smart move. Talk about making an awkward situation even worse. No, she has other things in mind.

The ladies room comes into view, and she almost throws herself through the door to separate herself from the room Marek is currently occupying. The sexual tension is thick like butter, and her bottom lip is raw as she continues nibbling away at it. Fortunately, the bathroom is just large enough for one person, and she flips the lock. She paces the floor in front of the mirror, contemplating what she's about to do. She's never been bold, and she's terrified of what will happen if this blows up in her face. What if she's reading all the signals wrong and he's not on the same page as her?

Stopping her pacing, she walks toward the mirror and really takes a look at herself. This could be one of those defining moments of her life, and she's going to jump completely in, feet first, ignoring the what-ifs. She smiles, says, "Fuck it," and finally follows through with a plan.

Tinley's heart races as she slowly walks back to the table. She's not bold. She doesn't take chances. She always lets life happen to her and pass her by, but something is telling her to finally put herself out there and go for it, like things could be different this time. At least she'll have tried something rather than sitting on the sidelines yet again. Marek's familiar black locks come into view as she gets closer and closer to the table. Her head is telling her to back out and not do it, but her gut is screaming at her to take a chance and just go for it.

He's focused on something on his phone, and his back is still to her as she walks right up to the table. The fact that he doesn't see it coming makes it that much more exhilarating. He jumps slightly in his seat as she leans down and softly kisses him on the cheek while simultaneously slipping her hand into his jacket pocket.

"Everything okay?"

She nods, smiles, and takes a sip of her brand new glass of wine that must have been refilled while she was gone. "I just thought I would leave a little present for you." She tips her head toward his jacket, and he scratches his chin while frowning. "Your pocket," she mouths, and his eyebrows rise with interest.

She watches as he dips his hand in, and she can tell the instant he finds his prize. Right away, he motions for the waitress to bring the check.

EIGHTEEN

*H*ave you ever had one of those moments that throws you back to being a teenager? That's exactly what this moment feels like, although Tinley wasn't your typical teenager so sneaking off somewhere semi-private to have sex wasn't something she ever partook in. Heck, she didn't even lose her virginity until college, and even then, it wasn't a very noteworthy experience. She definitely had no idea what she was doing, and the guy didn't know much more. He was a self-proclaimed Casanova, and the entire incident fell quite flat—literally, the dude couldn't keep it up to save his life—but that was her mistake in attempting to hook up with a guy who preferred smoking pot in his dorm room to actually going to class.

To be honest, every single memory of hers involving

sex has pretty much been a disaster. Maybe she's just destined for bad sex for the rest of her life. She's gotten pretty good at having a fun time with her B.O.B., so it's not like sex is really a necessity in her life anyway.

Marek leads the way, dragging Tinley through the dark parking garage until they end up beside his Highlander. It's a good thing he decided to drive it today rather than his motorcycle as usual. He presses up against her, and her back hits the cold metal of the car door. He leans his head down and presses his forehead to hers. "Are you sure you want to do this?"

"You're kidding me, right? You're trying to talk me out of this?"

"No." He shakes his head and opens the back door of his vehicle. "I'm really hoping you don't say no. I'm getting ready to blow my load in my pants if we don't actually do this, but it will permanently change things between us, so I just want to make sure you're sure. I'm not a complete dick, but fuck you've got me all worked up here, and I'd rather not have a repeat of blue balls again."

"Stop trying to be the voice of reason here Marek. You're ruining the mood. Let's go. Rock out with your cock out and all that." She turns around and hops in the back seat, hiding her bright red face. She can't believe those words just left her mouth. She's no prude, but that C-word has never left her lips before. It felt fitting for the mood, but now she feels like finding a hole to crawl into and die in. *Way to go on the awkward scale, Tinley.*

Marek lets out a small chuckle, but her embarrassment is quickly forgotten as he kisses his way down her face and nibbles lightly on her ear. She moans as he sucks right where her ear and neck meet and *holy wow*. The tingles engulf her body. He pushes her slightly, and she leans down, lying flat on his back seat. The aforementioned cock of his is rock hard and pressing against her stomach. Tinley's mind starts to race about his size and whether or not he'll be able to fit. It's hard to tell through his jeans, but he doesn't seem overly big; then again, all the guys she's been with have definitely been on the smaller side, or so she thinks.

Getting more confident than she's ever been before, she slides her hand down his body and cups him through the denim. Groaning, he rubs himself against her hand as he continues his trail of nips and kisses down her body. His rough, calloused hand runs along her collarbone and across her shoulder, sending chills down her spine. She continues rubbing her hand over his jeans, and he moans in her ear before biting down roughly on her shoulder.

"Marek, I want you," she moans breathily.

He removes her hand from him and holds both arms above her head. Gruffly he tells her, "Leave those there."

She can't even think past the next word out of her mouth as he pulls down the front of her dress and instantly takes one of her nipples into his mouth. His tongue swirls around the tiny nub over and over, and her breathing quickens. She's panting heavily and never knew how intensely pleasurable having her nipples played with could be. With a pop, he releases her and sits up. He pushes her dress up over her waist, and the cold air on her skin reminds her of the panties currently tucked away in his pocket.

She starts to say something but her words come out gurgled as Marek forces her right leg out as far as it will go and dives forward. Her legs start to clench up at the thought of what she knows he's about to do. This is, for the most part, no man's land. The pothead attempted it when he couldn't get himself off, but it was awkward and uncomfortable—too much saliva and not enough pleasure. That was the first time she ever faked it, but not the last.

In one swift moment, his tongue is on her, and any thought of college boy goes completely out the window. Her breathing and sighs become animalistic as he swirls his tongue around and focuses right in on her clit. Her legs start shaking from being stretched so far apart, but the familiar coil in the pit of her stomach starts up and any cramping is long forgotten.

He alternates between tongue-fucking her, thrashing away at her clit, and flat-out kissing her. The combination of rough and gentle has her screaming at the top of her lungs, and she hopes beyond anything else that he never stops. He shoves one then two fingers inside her, curving them both slightly and hitting her sweet spot inside. That's all it takes before her orgasm is ripping through her body and the shockwaves rack her.

The intensity starts slowing down, but his attack on her body does anything but. He latches his mouth on her clit and sucks while flicking his tongue against it. Her whole body shakes as the familiar buildup starts again, and she's totally lost herself to all comprehension. Her breathing is hard and rough, and she's so incredibly close to that release. She's become a greedy woman who wants nothing but orgasms over and over again.

He slides one of the fingers out of her and runs it along toward her backside. *No, not happening.* That's an exit-only zone. She starts wiggling, but before she can get a word out, his finger slides right in, and she sees stars. If she thought her first orgasm was unbelievable, this one is mind-blowing. She completely lets go and lets her body take over as she feels everything. The waves continue hitting one after the other as her body greedily pulsates and sucks his fingers in deeper.

It isn't until she hears the familiar rip of the condom wrapper that she realizes he's moved away from her again. Her body continued riding out the waves, and she just barely came crashing back down.

"Do you know how incredibly fucking sexy you look and sound as you come? I could do that to you all day."

All embarrassment or shyness has completely disappeared and only left a bolder Tinley as she replies, "I'd be one hundred percent okay with that. Nobody, and I mean nobody, has ever done that for me before, and definitely not like that."

"Which part?" He lies back down and kisses her on the mouth. "Multiple orgasms or go down on you?"

"Both?"

He leans up and looks her in the eyes. "What do you mean both? Never?"

She shrugs slightly. "No guy has ever given me an orgasm before. I thought I was broken."

"You're definitely not broken. You've just been with the wrong guys."

"I get that—ahh."

Before she can finish her sentence, he slides right in with one swift movement and completely fills her up. It's been so long that the sudden fullness is slightly painful at first, but as he slides out and then back in, her body adjusts to his size quickly. Their mouths come together as he moves at a slow, leisurely pace.

"So good. So fucking tight."

She lets out a slew of gurgled moans as she lets herself feel every single place where they're connected.

"I'm almost there. Bring your hand down between us and touch yourself."

She starts to feel embarrassed at the thought. She's never been comfortable with the idea of masturbating, let alone touching herself in someone else's presence, but he pulls her hand down, and she slides her fingers against her clit. She moans out and moves her fingers faster and faster at a steady pace. She didn't even know it was possible, but the familiar buildup starts again.

Marek grunts and asks, "Are you there?"

Tinley picks up the pace, and without even realizing it, she starts yelling, "I'm coming. I'm coming."

Everything goes dark as she closes her eyes and lets her body take over. It goes on for what feels like minutes, hours, maybe days even, and then she starts crashing back down to earth off of the most incredible high her body has ever experienced.

Holy shit. She takes it all back and then some. If that is what she's been missing this entire time, there is no way in hell she can go back to the misery of bad sex. Whatever that was...*just wow.* You read about epic sex in *Cosmopolitan* or romance novels, but she always assumed it was exaggerated. No boy or man has ever given her an orgasm before, let alone multiple, and if that's how Marek performs cramped in a car, what the hell does he have in store for her when they're actually in a bed?

NINETEEN

There's one thing that has been bugging Tinley since the night of their speed-dating date, and she's finally gotten the courage to ask her question—not so much courage that she'll ask him face to face, but enough for a text. She types it up quickly and sends it before she talks herself out of it.

Me: So, I never asked...you know why I was there, but why were you?

Marek: Why was I where?

Me: Speed dating. Doesn't really seem like your kind of thing.

She waits impatiently as the three little dots pop up on the screen and disappear a few times. She's about ready to send him another text when his message finally comes through.

Marek: I got tired of being alone.

She has absolutely no idea how to respond to that. Here's this guy who puts on a tough-guy front at work all the time, but that's just a portion of who he really is. She gets it. He has all this pressure on him to ensure that everyone around him is doing well at their jobs because it's his job on the line if they don't. To be honest, that's exactly why she's never pushed herself enough at work; she doesn't want to be management, doesn't want the stress that comes with it and can't imagine having that feeling every day. No, she'd rather just go to work, get her job done for the day, and leave. For her, work stays within the walls of the call center, and she can definitely see how that wouldn't apply to Marek.

Me: So why are you alone? I don't mean that in the way it comes out, but you're not exactly struggling in the looks department. It seems like women would be throwing themselves at you.

Marek: It's more complicated than
that.

Ugh. She tosses her phone down onto her bed in frustration. That's such a non-answer and all it does it annoy her.

Me: Then uncomplicate it for me.
Come on, we're being honest here.
Just talk to me.

She waits for the dots to appear, but they never do. The idea that she pushed him too far and he won't want to talk to her again crosses her mind and she almost sends him another text message to tell him he doesn't have to tell her anything, but then her phone starts ringing and his name comes up on her screen.

Without hesitation, she answers the call, and his voice comes across the line. "Where do you want me to start?"

"Anywhere you want to. I want to be here for you, but I don't know how to do that."

He sighs on the other end, and she can just picture him leaning his head down and running his hand through his hair. He tends to do it a lot when he's frustrated, and she wonders what's so difficult about this conversation for him. He's obviously experiencing some strong feelings.

"Five years ago, my best friend died."

It's not the response she was expecting at all, but she

stays silent, realizing how hard whatever he is about to say is for him.

"We grew up together. Cassie was the girl next door, and our parents always assumed we would end up together—get married, have kids, the whole nine yards—but I never saw her like that. It honestly never even crossed my mind. I loved her and wanted to protect her, but then ten years ago, she was diagnosed with cancer. To say I didn't take it well is an understatement. I completely rearranged my life and schedule for her. Every doctor's appointment, every chemo treatment—no matter what, I was there. She fought hard, harder than I would have had the strength to do myself, and she beat it."

His voice chokes up on the last sentence and Tinley's heart drops. There's more to this story, and Tinley doesn't know if she's ready to hear what else he has to say. There can't be a happy ending, or else he would be living it.

The tears in his voice are strong when he continues his story. "She went into remission, and I finally decided to pull my head out of my ass. After spending all that time together and being her support person, I finally saw her in a new light. We had a little too much wine one night to celebrate the anniversary of her being cancer free, and we finally crossed that line. It was more than I could have ever imagined it being. I couldn't believe all the time I had wasted and vowed to never waste a single minute with her."

Tinley quietly sobs, knowing where the story is

heading. Marek's voice is heavier and heavier with each word slipping from his mouth, and he no longer hides the sobs, letting the tears fall freely.

"I made plans to spend the rest of my life with Cassie, but not even one month after finally seeing what everyone else around us saw, her cancer was back. It was stronger than ever, and she didn't have it in her to fight anymore. I was so angry with her. She was just giving up on life, and I didn't want to let her go. She finally convinced me it was the right thing for her, and I had to be strong for the both of us. Watching her go through that as her energy levels dropped and she couldn't get out of bed near the end broke me. I pretty much gave up on life that day."

That's when the dam breaks free. Everything Marek was holding in releases and Tinley cries on the phone right along with him. She cries for Cassie losing her life at such a young age, cries for Marek for the major heartbreak he suffered and the fact that he might not ever get over it, and she cries for herself, wondering if she'll ever be enough for him or if he'll always be haunted by the ghost of his first love.

TWENTY

*T*inley rolls over in bed, and her phone lights up with a notification on her nightstand. After talking with Marek earlier, she found herself completely drained and exhausted. She went to bed a lot earlier than usual, not mentally prepared to process everything he told her over the phone.

Marek: Open your door.

What? That doesn't make any sense. Why would he text her that in the middle of the night? Well, the clock on her phone says it's not even ten yet, so it's not quite the middle of the night, but still. Curiosity gets the better of her, and she quietly slips out of her bedroom. All the lights in their apartment are off, and there's no light coming from underneath Dakota's bedroom door, so she must already be asleep. Tinley tiptoes down the hallway and walks over to the front door.

Sure enough, he's standing on the other side, and he looks completely wrecked. His eyes are bloodshot, and his shoulders are slumped.

"What are you doing here?" she asks.

"I needed to see you."

She nods and pulls him in, closing the door and locking it behind her. Grabbing his hand, she leads the way to her bedroom. "Are you staying?"

He sits down on the bed, and his voice comes out completely dejected. "If you'll let me."

She doesn't want to get caught, but there's no way she can turn him away after the conversation they had. He needs her, and she's willing to give herself to him in any way that'll make him feel better.

She walks over to the bed and sits beside him. She wraps her arms around him and pulls him closer then he places his hand on her thigh and quickly slides it up. She usually wears an oversized T-shirt to bed, and tonight is no different. She didn't even think about putting pants on before answering the door, but now she's rethinking her wardrobe choice.

She puts her hand on his and stops him from taking it any further. "Marek, stop. We shouldn't be doing this."

He leans forward and nibbles on the bottom of her ear, and goosebumps cover her entire body. His hand continues its exploration up her thigh, and his fingers slide over the front of her panties. She moans out as he applies pressure to her clit and runs his finger in a circular motion. She throws her head back and almost gives in to the feelings, but knows she shouldn't be doing this. She quickly stands up and steps away.

"I can't do this. After tonight, I feel like we both really need to consider what our future looks like, and I don't know if you're ready to be in a romantic relationship."

He stands up and stalks toward her like a lion going after its prey. A shoot of desire goes straight to her core, and she doesn't know how much longer she can keep pushing him away. She crosses her legs to curb her feelings, but it does nothing to help. He wraps his hand around her neck and places a small kiss on her lips. "Tinley, it's been four years since Cassie died. I've been mourning her loss this entire time, and I never contemplated the idea of moving on, but with you, things are different. I'm feeling things I've never felt before, and tonight when we talked on the phone, I was finally able to release everything I've been holding inside. I want this with you. I want us."

Her resolve was weak before, but now he's completely smashed anything she was holding back out of the water. He slams his mouth down onto hers, and Tinley moans as Marek runs his hands down her body then hoists her up onto the small desk behind them. Reaching under her shirt, he slides her panties down, leaving her wide open for the taking. Without hesitation, he immediately pulls down his sweatpants and slams right into her. She moans out at the sudden intensity, and he muffles her cries with his mouth. She can't tell if it's the emotions floating around them or if something about tonight is different, but she doesn't get long to contemplate as he slams into her again. She wraps her legs around his waist then he carries her from the desk to the bed and gently lays her down. Their grunts and groans are lost in their passionate kisses as he continues sliding in and out of her.

Their movements and sounds are animalistic as Marek picks up his speed. He's chasing after his release like a glass of water in the desert. He roughly rips her shirt off her body, and his mouth immediately locks onto her nipple. She throws her head back as the intensity almost brings her right to the brink.

His voice comes out rough and raspy as he asks, "Are you almost there?"

She moans in response as he pushes her legs up onto his shoulders and he sinks even deeper inside of her. She's completely full of him, and he's positioned at just the right angle to hit her right where she needs him over and over again. She loses herself and just lets her body take over and feel everything he's giving her. It's not long before he's grunting out his release and he collapses on top of her.

After a minute, he leans up and gently kisses her on the lips and asks, "Did you have yours?"

She turns her face away slightly and just nods her head, not wanting him to get a chance to look into her eyes and see the truth. Tonight, was about him and she doesn't want to make a big deal over her lack of orgasm.

"Tinley?"

When she doesn't respond, he turns her face toward his and looks in her eyes. "Fuck, I'm a dick. Why didn't you say anything?"

She shrugs and smiles. "It's no big deal. I don't need to have one every single time. Don't worry about it."

"That's not how this works. I'm not the kind of asshole who's going to have sex with you and leave you out in the cold. If I say my girl gets an orgasm, you get an orgasm. I'll spend all night until my tongue is raw if that's what it takes to prove it to you."

Her entire face to turns bright red and she looks at him completely stunned. Never in her life has a man been concerned about what she gets out of it when it comes to sex. If things ever end between her and Marek, she'll be ruined for all future relationships. That's for sure. She'll just have to go to a nunnery because there's no way she could find somebody better.

"Hold on, I want to change positions."

Tinley nods and starts to roll over, but Marek slightly tugs on her hips and starts rolling the opposite direction. In all of the push and pull from both sides, he puts a little extra force into it, and Tinley slides right off the bed and slams down on the floor.

"Shit, are you okay?"

She lets out a small grunt and flails out flat on her back. She can't decide which is worse: the pain radiating from her ass where she hit or the fact that she's lying completely naked on her bedroom floor. Rather than think about either, she starts cracking up laughing.

Banging comes from the other side of her bedroom door, and she immediately covers her mouth with both hands.

"Tinley are you okay?"

She calms herself down long enough to get out, "Yeah, I'm fine. I just rolled out of bed."

"Do you need me to come in there and help you out?"

That is the last thing she wants. Besides, she doesn't think Dakota would really appreciate seeing a completely naked Marek in her bed. "No! I'm fine, just go back to bed."

"Are you sure?"

"Yep. Good night."

"Night."

She stays on the floor for a bit then Marek swoops down and puts her back on the bed. Rather than joining her on the bed, he heads into her bathroom. The sink turns on and off again before he comes back to her on the bed. She's shocked to see a wet washcloth in his hand, and she's about to ask him what he's doing when he gently starts cleaning her up. She's never had someone do this with her before, and she honestly has no idea how to feel about it.

"Sorry about that. We probably should have discussed birth control methods, but I wasn't really thinking about that at the time. Are you on the pill?"

She has no idea what he's talking about until it dawns on her that they didn't use a condom. She's never had complete skin to skin contact with any man like that before and knows now why things felt so different. So much better and she wants to have that same connection with him every single time.

She goes into slight panic mode when his last question hits her. They just had sex completely unprotected. Shit. She shakes her head and replies, "I'm not, I've never had a reason to be."

He looks slightly pained, and he opens and closes his mouth multiple times before he says, "I don't want to be the kind of guy who tells you what to do with your own body, but would you consider going on the pill? After what we just did, I don't think I could use a condom with you ever again."

She smiles and almost laughs because they are on the exact same page with each other on that one. She nods and replies, "I was planning on making an appointment with my doctor tomorrow. Consider it done."

He kisses her on the forehead and huffs out, "Thank fuck," before hopping out of the bed to get rid of the dirty washcloth. He's only gone for a few seconds before he slides back in and pulls her back to his front and she sighs in contentment.

The mood has officially been killed so no more sexy

times tonight, but she feels just as good being wrapped up in his arms.

"I want to take you on a date."

She rolls over so they're facing each other and says, "We've already been on dates before."

"No, a real date. I want to pick you up and bring you flowers, take you out to a nice dinner and just get to know each other. I want to take work out of it, take our normal life stressors out of it, just you and me. What do you think?"

"I think you've already got me, no need to try to impress me."

"Good to know where we stand, but this isn't about that."

Tinley notices his change in demeanor and realizes how serious he is about this. If there's one thing she isn't going to do, it's pass up the opportunity for a romantic date. She wasn't lying when she told him she wasn't going anywhere, but can the same be said for him? There are no guarantees in this life, and you have to take opportunities when they come to you.

"Okay, let's go on a date then."

He smiles for the first time since arriving and kisses her lips. She rolls back over so her back is to his front, and his breathing quickly evens out as he falls asleep. As she lies there awake in his arms, she can't help but wonder if everything he said earlier is true. Is he really ready to move on with her? She doesn't know how she would be able to handle things if they did end up breaking up. They haven't been together for long, but her heart has already become more attached than she anticipated. She closes her eyes, and before sleep can take her, she tries to stop worrying and trust that everything will happen the way it's supposed to.

TWENTY-ONE

*N*ot long after they woke up this morning, Marek went home with plans to pick her up later for their date tonight. That was hours ago and Tinley has been sitting on the couch staring at her turned off television ever since. Last night felt like a turning point in their relationship, but she still feels so confused about everything. She hasn't had anyone to talk to about their entire relationship, and it's been driving her crazy.

Normally Dakota would be the person she would turn to in this kind of situation, but she hasn't seen her best friend all day, but that's kind of become her M.O. lately. Things between the two of them have been more distant, and Tinley has been so wrapped in everything with Marek that she hasn't really taken the time to find out what's going on with her roommate. She knows she should probably reach out to Dakota and find out what's going on with her but she can't go on her date tonight with all of this uncertainty. So instead she does the next best thing.

When her sister answers the door, Tinley is shocked. It has been a few weeks since the last time they saw each other, but still, her appearance is pretty rough. Her hair is piled high up on her head, and her eyes are completely sunken in with black circles underneath them. She can't tell with her oversized T-shirt, but it looks like her belly has doubled in size too. "I don't mean to sound like a bitch, but Tara you look like shit."

"Don't remind me of how much sleep I am losing right now. Whoever spread the lie that you should catch up sleep while you're pregnant before the baby comes has obviously never been pregnant before."

Tinley just shrugs. Isn't that how it is though? Get extra sleep at night and take naps during the day? That would make the most sense to her, but then again, she's never been pregnant before. "Should I know what that means?"

"Between the crazy pregnancy dreams and the frequent trips to the bathroom, I get at most two hours of sleep at a time. Hell, once I pop this little girl out I'll get longer stretches of sleep than I am right now. At least then I won't have a baby applying all of its weight and pressure to my bladder anymore."

That sounds exhausting and not something Tinley wants to experience herself anytime soon. She feels bad for coming over unannounced like this and asks, "Should I leave and let you nap?"

"Did you not hear anything I just said? Just come in, you're already here."

Tinley starts to hesitate, but Tara grabs her by the arm and drags her inside anyway. She does need help figuring everything out, so she doesn't protest too much when her sister drags her into the living room. She sits down in her recliner and motions for Tinley to take a seat in the room. For being so far along in her pregnancy one thing can definitely be said for her house. It's still impeccably cleaned as it always is. Tara is a bit of a neat freak, and Tinley can't help but wonder if some of the exhaustion affecting her sister is because she won't let herself relax at all.

"So, what's going on? You never come over."

She takes a deep breath and asks, "Do you remember Marek? The guy I work with?"

"How could I forget. What about him? Did he do something to be mean to you?"

"No, nothing like that. He was actually one of my dates for the speed dating thing. And well we've been seeing each other ever since."

"Okay?"

This is the part where it gets kind of awkward. There's added drama on their relationship, and she's not sure if that's something her sister would understand. She pauses for a moment and then just spits it out. "It's kind of a secret. He's a supervisor at work and could get into serious trouble for dating me even potentially lose his job, so even Dakota doesn't know."

"Well are things serious or are you just hooking up? Please tell me you've gone there and that it's amazing. I haven't had sex in a month because it's so uncomfortable at this point Clark is paranoid and thinks he'll stab the baby in the head with his dick."

Tinley cringes. That is not the kind of thing she wants to picture at all. She shakes her head and says, "First off, I really don't need to be hearing about yours and Clark's sex life or lack of. And second, I'm making an appointment on Monday to go on the pill, so yeah I'd say things have gotten pretty serious."

"I'm not going to try and understand what kind of friendship you and Dakota have that you can't trust her enough to tell her about your relationship, but we'll save that conversation for another day. Outside of that, if things are getting serious what's going on? Why are you here?

"We had kind of an intense night last night. He was in love with his best friend, and she died of cancer. That was four years ago, and he hasn't been with anyone since then. I'm just worried that I won't be enough and he's not ready for a relationship."

Tara mulls that over for a minute and then asks, "Did you ask him about it?"

"He said he was ready and that he wants to be with me. But I don't know what if that's not true."

"I think you need to stop second guessing things. If

he says he's ready for a relationship and he wants to be with you, why are you questioning it? Has he given you any reason to believe that he wouldn't be one hundred percent truthful with you so far?"

She shakes her head because Tara's right. This entire time Marek has been forthcoming about everything. This is her own insecurities talking and has nothing to do with him at all. She's just using that as an excuse when in reality she doesn't feel like she's good enough for him. She's always considered herself plain and unremarkable which is why she's never pursued anything career wise or really in all aspects of her life. Being twenty-nine working the same entry level position, still living with a roommate, and never getting seriously involved with someone, that's all been her doing. She's in a rut with her own life, and the only person she has to blame for that is herself.

"What's going on in that head of yours?"

Tears drip down from Tinley's eyes as she looks at her sister. "My life is kind of shit."

"I wouldn't say that."

"No, it is. I'm stuck in this horrible rut of watching my life pass me by, and it's all my own doing. I haven't done anything to be proud of, and it's all because I told myself I wasn't good enough. I've been second guessing this entire relationship with Marek because I've been telling myself he'll leave me eventually. How messed up is that? I sabotage my own life because I don't think I'm enough."

"So, what are you going to do about it?"

"I'm going to go home and get ready for the date that my gorgeous boyfriend is taking me on. Because I am good enough and I need to stop looking for issues where there aren't any."

"Damn right you are. Tinley, you know I love you, and I want nothing but the best for you. But you are only as capable as you believe you are. I know you could do anything you want to in this world, but you have to want it and tell yourself you can actually do it. Stop second guessing yourself and let yourself live. Truly live."

And then the damn really breaks free. Tinley and Tara never really had supportive parents growing up. It wasn't like they are bad people or anything like that, they just weren't involved or very encouraging. They had their own lives to worry about and never really took the time to make sure their children turned out okay outside of providing them food and shelter.

With a little extra effort, Tara pushes herself up and out of her chair and makes her way over to the couch where Tinley is breaking down. She wraps her arms around her and calms down her sobs. "I didn't mean to make you cry."

Tinley calms herself down and stops her sobs in order to tell her sister what's going on. "No, you don't get it. These are happy tears. I didn't even realize what I've been doing this entire time. I could have completely sacrificed an amazing relationship because of my own stupid head. I obviously have a lot to think about for everything else in my life, but I'm not going to ruin things between Marek and myself. I want to see where this goes."

"Good, I'm happy for you. You deserve to be truly happy."

And that's what Tinley takes with her as she leaves her sister's apartment to get ready for her date. She wants to be happy, and there's nothing standing in the way from Marek and her truly being happy together.

TWENTY-TWO

*T*inley's hands shake as applies her eyeliner. She doesn't know why she's so nervous. Sure, she had some nerves before the speed dating event and again the night when she and Marek finally saw each other face to face, but this is different. They've already been dating, albeit in secret, so what makes tonight so special? She ignores that little voice inside her head that tells her it's actually real now and that's why she's tense. She finishes off her makeup and gives herself one last look in the mirror when her phone goes off.

Marek: I'm outside.

The butterflies within her start turning into bats at the excitement. When Marek mentioned taking her on a real date, he wanted to do the whole nine yards including picking her up at her front door, but with Dakota around, that wouldn't have worked out. So, he agreed to wait in the parking lot for her. She peeks out of her bedroom door and hears her roommate talking on the phone in her bedroom. With her heels in hand, she makes a mad dash for the front door. Shutting it behind her, she puts her shoes on and makes her way over to her waiting date.

"Wow, you look amazing."

Her entire neck and face get hot, and she can imagine the redness building up in her skin. The look on his face alone is enough to make her drop her clothes right here in the parking lot, but they have a date to go on, and she's not about to ruin that. "Thank you. You look pretty incredible yourself."

And he absolutely does. She can't deny how turned on she is right now. He's got on a pair of nice black slacks and a button-up shirt. Just like the day she saw him with her sister, he has the sleeves rolled up, showing off those forearms in all their glory. She's tempted to run her hand along his arms but refrains from actually doing so. Might be taking it a little too far.

"So where are you taking me on this 'real date'?"

"Now if I tell you that, it wouldn't be a surprise, would it?"

"Marek Outlaw, are you getting romantic on me?"

His cheeks turn red, and she can honestly say she's never seen him embarrassed or blush before; she finds it very attractive. She leans over and places her hand on his cheek then pulls his face toward her. Her lips slide against his and just as quickly as she placed them, she pulls away.

"What was that for?"

"For being you."

She reaches down and tangles her hand with his own as they start walking toward his waiting vehicle. It's freshly washed on the outside, and when he opens the door to let her in, she notices the inside is equally as clean. He definitely went all out for this one. She smiles as he runs around the front of the car to get in on the driver's side. They haven't even left her apartment complex parking lot and already this has been the best date she's ever been on.

He hops in and takes off. With how secretive he was being, she half expected him to put a blindfold on her, but she's happy he didn't actually do that. As they're driving down the highway, he pulls her hand into his own and brings it up to his lips for a gentle kiss. He then lays it on the center console and doesn't let go. The simple things like that are absolutely perfect to her.

When they pull up to the valet outside the restaurant, she is completely shocked by where he's taking her. "Oh my gosh, how did you get a reservation here? They're always booked months in advance."

He offers a sly smile and says, "I have my ways."

As cheesy as it sounds, she feels like a princess being completely swept off her feet by a prince, and the sweeping is going way better than she ever could have imagined. The host leads them to a private table near the back of the restaurant. It's completely sectioned off in its own little room, and the music playing drowns out the noise from outside. There's already a bottle of wine chilling in a bucket next to their table and a basket of bread sitting in the middle. The host announces that the waiter will be in shortly with their first dish and exits the room.

Tinley's eyes are wide at all the opulence of their date, and she demands answers. "Seriously, what is going on here? How did you make all of this possible?"

He shrugs and simply asks, "Truth?"

She nods her head vigorously, eager for an answer.

"I own part of the restaurant." Her eyes go wide, but before she can ask anything, he continues. "One of my friends from college owns Big House Bookstore. It didn't always have the bar in the back, and when he got the idea to create it, he couldn't get a small business loan. I offered a chunk of my savings to him and became an investor. I don't have anything to do with the actual operations, but I receive a modest check every month. When business over there became profitable, he decided to step up his game and open this restaurant. Even though he didn't need the money this time around, he asked if I wanted a piece of the pie and I invested again."

She sits on that information for a bit and is completely shocked. If he's made such incredible business decisions, why does he stay at the call center? "I just have one question for you."

"Why don't I quit my job?"

She nods and laughs. Either he already knows her really well, or it was a predictable question—probably a little bit of both.

"I like the stability of the regular income. I rely on what I make from the call center to pay for all my everyday expenses. All the bar and restaurant money goes into savings for a college fund." He picks up the water glass in front of him and takes a drink.

"So you want to have kids someday?"

He chokes on the water in his mouth, and his eyes go wide. "Yeah, don't you?"

"I used to think I didn't, but I think that had more to do with not being in a relationship with anyone more than anything else. Now the idea is starting to grow on me."

There's a lull in the conversation as the waiter brings plate after plate of delicious food. Tinley can't remember the last time she had such a good meal, and afterward, she is stuffed. She can barely move, but she doesn't regret a minute of it. In fact, she would go back in time just to savor and enjoy every single bite again.

Marek comes around to her side of the table and slides her chair out to help her up. He brings her hand up to his mouth, and gives her a gentle kiss before leading her outside of the restaurant. She starts walking toward the valet and with a gentle tug he leads her away toward a park across the street. It's a little chilly outside but not incredibly unbearable, but she has to ask him anyway.

"Are we going for a walk?"

He smiles down at her and says, "Have a little patience. You'll see soon enough?"

"You mean the dinner wasn't our entire date? What else could you have planned?"

Marek continues smiling which does nothing but drive up Tinley's anxiety. She has no idea what else could be going on when they suddenly stop walking. And there, right in front of them is a freaking horse-drawn carriage. Including a blanket and a chilling bottle of wine. How the heck did she win the boyfriend jackpot?

Her mouth drops open as he drags her over to the carriage. "Are you kidding me right now? How is it possible that you just took the most perfect date I've ever been on and escalated it to ultimate level? Sorry for the cliché, but is this real life right now?"

He leans down and gives her a gentle kiss on the lips and asks, "So I did good?"

All she can do is nod her head as he helps her into the carriage. They snuggle together underneath the blanket and he hands her a glass of wine. Perfection. That is the only word she can think of to describe this date. Absolutely perfection.

She turns toward him and smiles. "Thank you so much for the most perfect night I've ever had. I would never have guessed you were a secret romantic inside."

"It's not really a secret, I've just never been in a relationship with someone I could spoil before now."

"Are you trying to make me fall in love with you?"

"Is it working?"

"Possibly. The jury is still out on that one."

He leans over and pulls her in for a kiss. She one hundred percent lied because she knows with all her heart she has already fallen head over heels in love with this man.

TWENTY-THREE

*T*oday was rough. For some reason, they suddenly had a surge of business at work, and the phones were ringing off the hook. Tinley completely missed her afternoon break because she couldn't break away from her phone and she didn't get a chance to talk to Marek at all today. All of the supervisors were taking calls to help out with the call volume. To say the day was madness is a complete understatement. On the upside, she was able to book quite a few vacation packages and will be getting a hefty bonus next month. Her brain literally feels like mush, and she's been sitting on the couch staring at the wall since she got home. She took her shoes off and just collapsed right after walking in the door.

Tinley is contemplating ordering a pizza when her

phone lights up with a text notification. Oddly enough, it's a text from her roommate, and she looks at the time on her phone. Dakota should have been home at least an hour ago. She opens the message and is surprised by what she finds waiting for her.

Dakota: Hey, I know this is super last minute but I just wanted to let you know I'm going out of town. Well actually, I've already left.

Me: Thanks for telling me?

Dakota: Yeah, I know. Sorry about that. I came home at lunch and packed a bag. I've got some stuff going on this weekend so I just wanted to let you know I won't be home at all.

Me: What kind of stuff?

Dakota: Can't talk about it right now. Actually, I'm getting on a plane so I'll see you on Monday.

A plane? This whole situation is weird and so

completely uncharacteristic of her roommate. She can't even remember the last time Dakota was on a plane, or if she's *ever* flown anywhere. Sure, they've talked about taking vacations together, but they're both always too broke to actually take that thought process seriously. So, instead, they just dream together and plan trips they'll never take. It can actually get pretty depressing, now that she thinks about it.

She's got the whole place to herself for the entire weekend, and there's only one person she wants to spend it with.

Me: Dakota is going to be gone all weekend. Feel like having a sleepover?

Marek: Gone? Where is she going?

Me: I don't know, she's being super weird and mysterious. All I know is she told me she won't be home all weekend and not to worry about her.

Marek: Has she ever done anything like this before?

Me: Nope, never, but I don't want to waste my weekend speculating

on what my roommate is doing.
Do you want to come over? Or I
could pack a bag and come over
there.

Marek: I'll come over there. Just
give me a few hours. I've got
some stuff going on that I need
to finish up and then I'll be
over.

Me: Sounds good. Can't wait to see
you.

Marek: You too.

She puts her cell phone down on the couch and can't help the giddy smile on her face. Everything about that man makes her smile, and now she gets to spend the entire weekend with him, completely uninterrupted. It's only then that she realizes he'll be here in a few short hours and the apartment is a disaster, *and* she hasn't shaved. She immediately jumps up from the couch, forgetting about the blanket she has wrapped around her legs. She tumbles to the ground and her butt slams down on the floor—hard. She whimpers in pain, but if anything, she's just happy she missed the coffee table. That would have been tragic. She stands up, now in full freak-out mode because she needs to get everything ready.

The knock on her front door echoes throughout her apartment and Tinley can't contain her excitement. An entire weekend of alone time with Marek, no sneaking around at all—they can just be together and act like they're in a normal relationship for once. Maybe she'll actually convince him that it'll be fine to tell Dakota about them dating. It's not like she's going to spill the beans to anyone at work. She's her roommate, and Tinley trusts her with everything. They're practically sisters.

With one last glance in the mirror, she heads out to answer the door. It's so weird—she was never the kind of girl who got excited and would primp before a guy came over. She runs quietly so he can't hear her feet pounding on the hardwood then straightens her shirt before opening the door.

"Hey."

She leans against the doorjamb and immediately undresses him with her eyes. Licking her lips, she can't help but feel excited by the idea of weekend-long marathon sex. She's never really cared about her lack of sex life before, but now with Marek, she's absolutely addicted. "Hi."

"Can I come in?"

"Yeah, sorry." She shakes her head and steps to the side so he can enter. "I'm just super nervous for some reason. I don't know what's going on with me."

He enters the apartment and closes the door behind him. He drops his duffle bag on the floor next to their feet and instantly wraps his arms around her, pulling her toward him. He plants his lips down on hers, and she lets out a small sigh as she relaxes into him. His hands work their way down her backside, and he squeezes on her butt, forcing them together even closer. He runs his tongue along her bottom lip, and she immediately opens up for him. As soon as their tongues tangle, she runs her hands through his hair and moans as his arousal becomes evident on her stomach.

He pulls away and places his forehead against hers, and both of their breaths come out labored. "Better?"

Better? What's he talking about? "Huh?" she responds in a daze, forcing herself up onto her tiptoes to continue the very hot make-out session.

"You said you were nervous, so I was distracting you from your nerves. Are you better now?"

She pulls his head down. "I'll be much better as soon as you stop talking and put your mouth back on mine."

He chuckles and starts to say something else in response, but Tinley beats him to it and pulls his lips back down to her own. She has every intention of using this weekend to its fullest and doesn't want to waste a single minute with talking, at least for now.

He pushes back from her slightly, and Tinley starts to pout. "What's the rush? We have all weekend. Have you eaten yet? Maybe we can start with some dinner?"

"Ugh, why do you always have to be so adulty about stuff? Can't we just skip dinner and go straight to dessert?" Of course, her traitorous stomach decides to give her away and grumbles. So maybe she hasn't eaten anything either and is ridiculously starving, but who can think about food when there's a gorgeous man standing in front of you? Definitely not Tinley.

He chuckles and replies, "Normally I would be completely on board with that idea, but I'm actually really hungry, and it sounds like you are too, so we should probably do that first."

"If I must feed you, I guess we'll just start there, but as soon as we're done eating, you're mine."

She makes good on her word. As soon as the last bite of food from his plate touches his mouth, she's instantly on him. This time he doesn't put up a fight, and she thanks the gods over and over again for bringing this man into her life.

TWENTY-FOUR

The heat from the sun instantly warms Tinley's face as she wakes up, and the smile on her face is permanently etched there. She knows she's not alone as the scent of Marek wraps itself around her like a warm fuzzy blanket. She stretches her arms above her head and rolls over, opening her eyes and finding that he's already awake beside her. He's lying on his side and has his head leaning on his hand. When she woke up yesterday morning, he was in the exact same position. "Are you going to watch me sleep every time we're in bed together?"

"You make it sound like I'm doing something creepy. I haven't been awake for that long, you know."

"Sure creeper, that's what you want me to believe. I know the truth—you're secretly plotting my demise while I sleep."

"Yeah, and where would that get me?"

She contemplates for a minute, dramatizing her thought process by tapping her finger against her chin. With a shrug, she replies, "I couldn't tell you. It's not like we're married and there's a life insurance policy at stake."

He releases a laugh and looks at her like she's crazy. "Somebody has watched one too many Lifetime movies."

"Have you watched some of those? The storylines can get intense, and the really crazy thing is that some of them are true stories."

"You sound like my mother right now."

Well, that was definitely not what she expected to come out of his mouth. Her nose scrunches up, and she almost has to roll away from him. That should never be something that comes up while they're in bed together. She's not one for making rules for the bedroom, but that should be a given.

"You really want to talk about your mother while we're in bed together? Just think about that for a minute."

"Good point. I won't make the same mistake twice."

"Sounds like a solid plan—and speaking of solid plans, is little Marek happy to see me this morning?"

"I don't know, maybe you should find out for yourself."

He pulls her toward him for a good morning kiss,

and they proceed to find out just how excited he is to see her.

"Do you have any tissues in your purse?"

Tinley never knows what she has in that thing. She always shoves stuff in there and then forgets about it later. It's a good thing she doesn't have Hermione's bag, she'd probably find a way to shove everything she owns in there. She goes digging around in the bottomless pit and her hands land on an old napkin. It's not crumbled, so good chances that it hasn't been used before.

"Here you go."

She passes it over to Marek, and he brings it up to his face but stops and smirks.

"So, who's Jared? Should I be worried you're going to be leaving me for this faceless guy? Or do you have a purse full of these things and poor Jared didn't make the cut?"

Jared? She has no idea what he's talking about. She reaches for the napkin and quickly snags it from his hand. Sure, enough there's a phone number under Jared's name. What the heck? And then it dawns on her where exactly this came from. She can't help but laugh because this definitely isn't a regular occurrence for her. Outside of rarely stepping foot into a bar, odds are more likely Dakota will get hit on than herself.

"That's from the Dating in the Dark night. The waiter gave me his phone number, and I never had any intention of using it. I actually completely forgot it was in there until just now."

She hates that their weekend is coming to a close. They just finished up the best lunch at a cute little soup shop near her apartment building, and they've been walking through the park since they finished. Her hands shake as they take a seat on a bench. She knows how she's been feeling about Marek lately, but it feels too soon, and what if he doesn't feel the same way? That's not the kind of rejection she would be able to handle, not after everything they've been through already. In the short amount of time they've been together as a couple, she has changed so much as a person, grown so much.

Turning toward him, she blurts out, "I really want to tell you something, but I don't want to make a fool of myself. So…I'm going to wait a little bit longer."

He suddenly stands up and pulls her up with him. "It's really getting late, and I should probably get going."

"Thank you for coming over this weekend. It was absolutely perfect."

She leans into his embrace and holds on tight. They didn't get a chance to talk about how they could move their relationship to the next step, but after this weekend, it's clear that's exactly what she wants to do. She's tired of hiding.

Marek leans his head down and plants a gentle kiss on her cheek. He tightens his grip on her and whispers in her ear, "Tinley, I love you too."

She squeezes him tighter and breaks down crying. Ugly tears force themselves down her face, and she can't hold back the sobs that start racking her body. Marek leans back slightly, and his eyes go wide at the destruction she's creating.

"Are you okay? Why are you crying?"

She barely calms herself down enough to get any words out. "I can't believe how beautiful and perfect that was. I love you so damn much, and you just solidified my feelings with your proclamation."

"So, these are happy tears?"

"So incredibly happy. I can't stop them, that's how happy I am."

He wraps his arms back around her body and pulls her in close. She continues sobbing into his chest, and it takes her forever before she's finally able to calm herself down. This man that she currently has herself wrapped around is her forever; she knows that now. He's been here right under her nose this entire time, and if it weren't for her sister and best friend pushing her, she would have never seen it. Now she can't imagine ever living her life without him. This is the epitome of perfection.

TWENTY-FIVE

*R*ecently, Tinley has been sucked into all the cheesy romance movies filling up her feed on Netflix. She was never a romantic movie kind of girl, but lately, she just feels in the mood for romance. Being with Marek has definitely brought out a different side of her. Plus, they keep popping up for her to watch. They might also keep showing up because she's watching all of them, but she's not one to question it. This latest one has her completely sucked in. A happily ever after seems pretty much impossible at this point, which means the ending is going to be over the top and epic. She gets giddy just thinking about it.

The two main characters are about to finally give in to their true feelings and share that first kiss when the front door to her apartment flies open. Tinley quickly pauses the movie and looks up as her roommate comes storming into the room. Her face is covered in tears, and her makeup is completely ruined. "Dakota are you okay? What's wrong?"

She just solemnly shakes her head and continues toward her bedroom. What the hell could have happened at work to have her this upset? She never gets upset about anything work-related. "I don't want to talk about it. Just drop it."

"But—"

"No, Tinley. I said drop it." Then she walks out of the room and slams her door.

The familiar sound of the lock clicking into place echoes down the hallway, and Tinley suddenly feels uncomfortable in her own home, almost like she's intruding on whatever is going on with her roommate. Rather than stick around any longer, she picks up her phone and sends off a quick text to Marek. Maybe they can get together.

> **Me:** Hey, what are you up to? Dakota just got home from work and she's acting super weird. I'd rather not be here right now. Do you care if I come over?

As soon as Tinley sends off the text, she contemplates what she just said. She and Marek haven't been together for all that long, but it's still kind of weird that she's never been to his place before. He's always coming to her instead. A few seconds later, her phone lights up with a notification, and she instantly feels let down.

Marek: Sorry, it's not a good time. Can we talk later?

Me: Yeah, sure.

She gets up from the couch and considers going into the kitchen to whip up a batch of cupcakes, but then she pauses. The old Tinley would make cupcakes every time she was bored, sad, or even hungry, but the new Tinley does not need someone else to keep her company to be happy. Instead, she decides she needs to go out and do something for herself for a change. Her hair and makeup are still fixed up from when she was at work earlier, but the yoga pants she currently has on won't cut it.

When she comes back out into the living room, she's pleasantly surprised to find Dakota standing there digging around in her purse. Her makeup is completely freshened up, and she's swapped out her flats for heeled boots and her T-shirt for a ruffled blouse.

"Dakota, where are you going?"

"Out. I need to get completely shitfaced. Are you coming or staying?"

She doesn't need someone to keep her company, but going to the bar with Dakota will definitely be a lot more fun than going by herself. Besides, it definitely seems like she could use a good cheering up, and hopefully, she'll tell her what the heck happened in the hour between Tinley leaving work and Dakota getting off for the day. And maybe she can finally figure out what she's been hiding. Even after the mysterious trip she took, Dakota has been completely quiet about what she's been doing on her laptop every night. Wordlessly, Tinley grabs her purse and keys and leads the way downstairs. As they head down, she pulls up the Uber app on her phone. It's sounding like it's going to be a long night, and she has a feeling neither one of them are going to be okay to drive after it's all over with.

Tinley lucked out that the password was exactly the same as last time. She figured she had a fifty-fifty chance that they constantly change it or keep it the same. Lucky for her, they don't change it, so it's not so secret after all— which reminds her, she never did get a chance to ask Marek why he didn't tell her the password to get in in the first place. It's possible that it didn't cross his mind because he doesn't have to use it when he comes here.

They step foot into the darkened room, and Dakota's eyebrows go up as she takes everything in. Tinley isn't nervous this time like she was before, so she's able to appreciate the atmosphere alongside her roommate, including the giant clawfoot tub in the middle of the room. How did she miss that last time?

"So, how did you find out about this place anyway?"

It seemed like a good idea to bring Dakota here, but now Tinley is seriously questioning her own judgment. Of course, her friend would want to know how she found out about the place. It's not like Tinley goes barhopping or trolls the internet looking for hip new places to go to. No, instead she spends most nights at home with a glass of wine, a cupcake, and Netflix. She's more yoga pants than high heels, that's for sure. She pretends like she doesn't hear her roommate's question and instead drags her off toward the bar so they can start drinking immediately; hopefully, Dakota will start spilling her secrets rather than the other way around.

"What do you feel like drinking? Should I get a menu from the bartender or do you know what you're in the mood for?"

"Alcohol. I don't care what's in it, I just need alcohol and a lot of it."

Okay, so it's going to be one of those nights. Tinley motions for the bartender to come over so she can place an order.

"What can I get started for you ladies?"

She can only remember the name of one drink from last time. She didn't get a chance to try it, but it sounded delicious. So, she orders those to start off with. "We'll each start with a Giggle Water, and if you could bring us a menu as well, that would be great." She motions to her roommate and says, "This one has no idea what she wants to drink but plans to drink a lot of it. She's upset about something but won't tell me what it is. I'm hoping some liquid courage will help loosen up those lips."

Dakota starts laughing as she takes a seat at the bar and looks up at all the liquor bottles lining the wall behind the bartender. "What the hell is a Giggle Water?"

"Just trust me, you'll like it."

Famous last words right there.

TWENTY-SIX

*T*inley yelps out in pain as she rolls over in bed. Never ever again is she agreeing to go out with Dakota to a bar. All that leads to is mistakes and hangovers—awful, horrible hangovers that are excruciatingly painful. On the upside, she's in her own bed, so no walk of shame, and she's in love with an amazing man, so no awkward morning conversation with a one-night stand. Good thing for silver linings and all that, but what she can't get behind is the sun blaring through her blinds. She definitely needs to invest in some blackout curtains.

She flops out flat on her back and assesses the damage done to her body because something definitely wrong. Starting at the bottom and working her way up, she wiggles one foot and then starts with the other but screams out a list of expletives. The pain radiates from her ankle all the way up her leg, and she curses her roommate and her need to get drunk last night. It's apparent that they both got way more than they bargained for.

Her bedroom door flies open, and Dakota comes charging in. "What's going on? Why did you scream?"

She attempts to sit up but loses all strength and flails back down onto the bed. "What the hell happened last night and what is wrong with my ankle?"

Tilting her head to the side, her roommate looks at her in confusion and then steps toward the bed. "I have no idea what you're talking about." She lifts the comforter on the bottom half of her body and screams out, "Holy shit! What the hell did you do to your ankle?"

"What are you talking—oh!" Sitting up, she pulls her covers all the way off and looks at the offending ankle. It's a rainbow of black, blue, and purple and has swollen up to twice its size. "Shit, Dakota. That doesn't look good at all."

"You're right. I'm going to go change my clothes, and we're going to the hospital." She picks up a pair of sweatpants and slippers and throws them at Tinley. "Here, maneuver these on and I'll be right back. We can piece together what happened last night on the way there."

"Fuck my life." She reaches for her phone on her nightstand to send a quick text to Marek and finds a few missed texts and one missed call from him.

Marek: Sorry about earlier. Is everything okay?

Marek: Are you mad at me? I'm sorry I couldn't talk earlier.

Marek: Tinley, call me. You've got me worried.

Serves him right for being too busy when she needed him. If she could have just gone over to his place in the first place, none of this would have happened. Now she has a busted ankle, and who knows how long she'll be out of commission. Feeling pathetic, she quickly types out a text and doesn't think before hitting send.

Me: I'm pretty sure I broke my ankle and I'm also pretty sure I'm never drinking with Dakota again, and it's all your fault.

He doesn't instantly send a reply, which sours her mood even more. Doesn't he know that she needs him right now? What else could be going on in his life that is so much more important? Nothing, that's what. Wallowing in her own personal pity party, she gently slides on her sweatpants, avoiding her ankle as much as possible. She whimpers out in pain but continues on. Fortunately, Dakota was smart enough to toss her slippers over, and she easily slides those on.

A couple minutes later, her best friend comes flying back to her room. "Okay, I've got the car warming up right now, and I pulled it around right outside the door. I'm going to help you up, and you can put all your weight on me."

Tinley starts to get up and Dakota freezes. "Wait! You need a sweatshirt." She runs over to Tinley's closet and grabs one, throwing it at her face.

She pulls it on over her head and watches as her roommate wears a hole in the floor. "Dakota! Stop pacing. You're starting to freak me out. Calm yourself down, it's just an ankle. It's not like I'm dying."

She turns toward her and instantly breaks down crying. "I'm so sorry. This whole thing is my fault. If I hadn't wanted to go out last night, we wouldn't have gotten wasted, and you wouldn't be broken right now."

Tinley can't remember much from last night, but she doesn't think they actually talked about whatever has been bothering Dakota. And she has a feeling this breakdown is probably more about that than the fact that Tinley may or may not have a broken ankle right now. Dakota has her breakdown for several minutes before helping Tinley out to the car. Before they take off, she shoots another text to Marek to at least let him know what's going on.

Me: I don't want you to be worried, but my ankle is in pretty bad

```
shape and Dakota is taking me to
the hospital to get it checked
out. I don't want to bother you
because    you    obviously    have
something going on, but I wanted
you to know just in case.
```

"Are you currently pregnant?"

Dakota starts cracking up laughing, and Tinley chuckles along with her then answers, "Uh, not that I know of."

The nurse looks from Dakota and back to Tinley. Obviously annoyed with the both of them, she asks her question differently, "Let me rephrase that: is it possible that you could be pregnant? You're about to get an x-ray, and while it's on your ankle, we still need to take extra precautions if you're pregnant."

Tinley looks over at Dakota, whose mouth is hanging wide open. She hasn't told her roommate about Marek yet or the fact that she's seeing anyone at all, and now is really not the time to have that conversation.

The nurse sees the reluctance on Tinley's face and turns toward Dakota. "Ma'am, I'm going to have to ask you to step outside for a moment."

"But—"

"It's okay Dakota, just do what she says."

Dakota purses her lips but nods. "Fine. I'm going to go get some coffee for both of us then I'll be back." She steps out of the room and heads down the hallway.

"Sorry, my roommate doesn't know I'm dating someone. She actually isn't too fond of him, and that's why I haven't told her. I'm pretty sure I'm not pregnant, but I don't really know what it feels like to be pregnant. I've been sexually active for a while now, maybe a few months or so...sorry, I don't remember the exact date. I am on the pill though, so I can't be pregnant, right?"

"Okay, when was the first day of your last period?"

Her mom always told her to keep track of things like that, but it never seemed important enough before. She also wasn't sleeping with anyone, so it wasn't a big deal if her period didn't come every month because there was no way she could be pregnant anyway. She looks up at the nurse and shrugs her shoulders.

The nurse hands her a cup and makes her go fill it up in the bathroom. She knows she should have some sort of feeling about this, but mostly she's just annoyed about her ankle. Hobbling to the bathroom to pee in a cup is not how she planned on spending her day—not that she really had any plans in mind, but Netflix and a cupcake sounds much better than this. With a rush order placed on the results of the test, Tinley has her answer within thirty minutes, and she doesn't have time to process before she's whisked off to get her x-ray.

"Sorry to break it to you, but looks like it's broken."

"Was that some kind of funny doctor humor with your pun there? And are you sure? Can I get a second opinion from another doctor? Maybe you're reading the x-ray wrong."

He looks mildly annoyed as he puts the x-ray back up on the light box thing and turns it on. Tinley doesn't really know what she's looking at other than seeing the outline of her leg and foot.

"Do you see that space right there?" He points to a spot near where she thinks her ankle is and nods her head. Turning back toward her, he says, "You're not supposed to have a space there. The bone is supposed to be attached in that spot, and your bone is fractured."

"Well shit."

He chuckles slightly and shuts the light off. "That's one way to put it."

He goes on to explain how long it's going to take to heal and the fact that she'll be stuck in a boot for some amount of time, but she ignores everything he says. A tall man with dark hair just walked by her door, and she could have sworn it was Marek, but if he were at the hospital for some reason, wouldn't he have told her?

TWENTY-SEVEN

*T*he frat boy corner, as Dakota and Tinley always refer to it, is surprisingly quiet today. Of course, she isn't used to working on a Saturday, but still, there's usually more excitement over there. Maybe their luck has run out, and they're struggling to bring in sales like everyone else in the office. Her curiosity gets the better of her, and she hobbles off to the bathroom, which takes her right by that section of the sales floor. What completely surprises her is the fact that Marek seems to be missing from his desk.

Jonah is getting up from his computer at the same time as she passes by, no doubt for one of his many smoke breaks, and she asks, "Hey Jonah, is Marek not in today? I thought it was mandatory for everyone on the phones to work today."

He shrugs and mumbles something under his breath about needing a smoke then continues walking past her. It's pretty freaking rude, but still, it doesn't change the fact that Marek didn't come in today. He never misses work, and she still hasn't heard from him since before she broke her foot. She's been out all week because of her stupid injury, and today was her first day back. She had been hoping to finally see Marek and talk about everything. The silence has been gotten annoying at this point; if he doesn't want to actually take their relationship somewhere, he needs to let her know and not do this stupid ghosting shit. What happened to him telling her he was a man and not into childish games?

She wanted to reach out so many times this week, but her pride got the better of her. He never responded to the last text she sent him before she went to the hospital and she doesn't exactly want to talk to him anyway other than in person with the news she has. But at this point, she's debating on whether or not she should tell him at all.

When she gets into the bathroom, she pulls her phone out of her hoodie pocket and immediately shoots off a text to him.

Me: Hey, didn't you have to work today?

She expects radio silence yet again but is pleasantly surprised when he immediately starts typing out a response. She's almost worried what he's going to say back to her since it's been over a week since the last time they talked.

> **Marek:** I'm sick and I stayed home. I should be all better by Monday though.

> **Me:** Oh no. Do you need me to get you anything?

> **Marek:** No. It's just a cold. I'm actually getting ready to take a nap. I'll talk to you later.

> **Me:** Feel better soon. Let me know if you need anything.

So, if she did see him at the hospital last weekend when she was there, it must have been because he was sick. Now she feels absolutely horrible for thinking he was just being a jerk and avoiding her when in reality he's been sick this whole time. He's probably been at home completely miserable and attempting to take care of himself. What kind of a girlfriend does it make her that she's been avoiding reaching out to him because she thought he was ignoring her? *Ugh.* Now look who's playing games and sounds like a toddler. Her hormones are turning her into a crazy person or something. She mentally berates herself and makes plans to bring him a nice care package later when she gets off work, which is only in a couple of hours since they have a half-day today.

After getting off work, Tinley immediately went to the soup place she and Marek went to the day he told her he loved her. What better way to make him feel better than a gentle reminder of their love for each other? It will also distract from how much of a jerk she's been this week. Fortunately, she just made a batch of cupcakes last night so she can grab some of those as well.

When she came flying through the front door of her apartment, her roommate was nowhere in sight, and she assumed Dakota was gone for the day. What she did not expect was to find her sitting on the couch when she came out of her bedroom after changing into a sundress. She wanted to feel pretty for once, even if she has to wear that damn boot.

"Where are you off to?"

"I have a friend who is sick, so I'm bringing h-her some cupcakes and soup." She almost said the wrong pronoun there, and that would have been a disaster. She feels kind of gross about still lying to Dakota about everything, but Marek has a lot to lose if anyone at work finds out they're together. He might not be her direct supervisor, but he's still a supervisor, and that's grounds for him to get fired.

"What friend? You don't have any other friends."

Shit. She didn't really think that one through at all. Of course Dakota is going to question her when she suddenly mentions a friend. Wouldn't she have already mentioned this person before? *Way to go.* "I, uh, met her during that speed-dating thing. We both laughed about how lame the thing was."

"And now you're close enough for you to take her soup when she's sick? Don't you think that's kind of weird?"

"Why do you care? I can have more friends than just you, geez."

The guilt hits Tinley almost immediately as she opens the front door and walks away after slamming it behind her. She didn't mean to get so defensive, but she can't risk Dakota finding out her secret until she and Marek figure things out. Which is why she doesn't care how sick he is. It's been long enough, and they have way too much to talk about. Whether or not he wants to see her, they're going to figure everything out today. Time—that's all she needs.

TWENTY-EIGHT

The butterflies in her stomach are flapping a million miles a minute. She knows she shouldn't be this nervous and excited, but something about Marek just sets her body on fire. Yes, the sex is mind-blowing, but it's more than that. He gets her, and for the first time in her almost thirty years of life, she feels it—the insane connection you can't describe, but when you have it, you know it's meant to be. Never in a million years did she think she would be thinking about who her soul mate is, but it's hard to deny what's so obvious.

It might seem slightly stalkerish that she found Marek's address with a quick internet search, but it's not her fault that it's really easy to cyberstalk people these days. The very first link that popped up was his address. The fact that he owns his own home means he has at least part of his life together, and that is a complete turn-on. Besides, he can't be too mad at her when he sees the treats she brought him.

Since the sun finally decided to pop up today and warm everything up a bit, her cute sundress is perfect, and the cupcakes and soup are safely tucked away in her wicker picnic basket. She's secretly hoping he's not super sick and will let her stay to nurse him back to health. For half a second, she contemplated wearing Dakota's nurse costume from last year's Halloween, but there's no way she would have easily left the house wearing it. Her roommate was already suspicious enough.

She pulls her car into the driveway and double-checks the address on her phone. Yep, definitely the place. It's an adorable craftsman-style house with stone and natural wood detailing, but her absolute favorite part is the oversized porch complete with a porch swing. This is the kind of house she could imagine herself living in—with a family, of course. She instinctually places her hand on her belly and butterflies fill her stomach. Maybe she should start looking for a new job. There's nothing really keeping her at the call center, and the pay isn't really worth it. She could find something different, and then they wouldn't have to hide their relationship anymore.

She eyes the porch swing again and can just imagine swinging all snuggled up with Marek on a hot summer night, sipping on lemonade. It sounds absolutely perfect. Completely set on telling Marek her plan to find a new place of employment soon, she knocks on the door. After a couple of minutes and still no answer, she's about to knock again but the front door swings open.

A little girl with dark raven long hair and bright blue eyes stands in front of her, wearing kitty pajamas. She looks Tinley up and down and tilts her head to the side. "Who are you? You're not my mommy."

The girl is absolutely adorable, but if she's the reason Marek is at home, why didn't he just say that? It's one thing for him to call in sick to work, but why did he tell her the same story instead of the truth?

"You're right, sweetie, I'm not your mommy. Is your Uncle Marek home?" She doesn't know if Marek has a younger sister or niece, but this little girl doesn't look much older than four, maybe five. If she's his younger sister, that's a huge age gap, so niece is more likely.

The little girl throws her head back and starts laughing hysterically. Her giggles are loud and overly exaggerated, but Tinley can't help but smile at happiness she's exuding. The little girl plops herself onto the floor sitting with her legs crossed and stops laughing long enough to say, "I don't have an Uncle Marek."

Maybe this little girl is a neighbor or friend's daughter? Although it seems strange that Marek would miss work to do a favor for somebody else.

Tinley crouches down so that she's at the same level as the girl and asks, "Oh, is he—"

"My daddy's name is Marek though, and my name is Luna. What's your name?"

To be continued...

Continue reading Tinley & Marek's story in
Sinking in the Shadows
Releases May 14th

PLAYLIST

"Floral and Fading" Pierce the Veil
"My Songs Know What You Did in the Dark" Fall Out
Boy
"Good Times" All Time Low
"Dirty Little Secret" The All-American Rejects
"The Only Difference Between Martyrdom and Suicide Is
Press Coverage" Panic! At the Disco
"Feel Good" Neon Trees
"Good to Be Alive (Hallelujah)" Andy Grammer
"Heartbeat" Mat Kearney
"How You Love Me Now" Hey Monday
"Into the Rest (Feat. Kellin Quinn)" Avion Roe
"Stupid for You" Waterparks
"I Wanna Go Out" American Authors
"Take Me To The Top" ONE OK ROCK
"Empire to Ashes" Sleeping with Sirens
"A Beautiful Lie" Thirty Seconds to Mars

ACKNOWLEDGEMENTS

Why are these always so hard to write? I always put off writing the acknowledgements until the very end and then I have to scramble. Procrastination at its finest ;)

As always, I have to start with a major thank to you my husband. He always puts up with my crazy when I'm working on a new book and I let stuff like house work and cooking go to the backburner.

To Aubrey. Pfft, like you didn't know you'd end up in here. We've only been friends for a couple of years, but dude it feels like we've been together for life. Seriously though, you're always the first person I think to talk to and you're always there for me. One of these days I'll convince you to move to my side of the world.

To Megan. Dude! You completely nailed it on the cover. You were patient while I was indecisive and wishy washy. You didn't even bat an eyelash when I had you change things five hundred million times. I owe you all the pizza and coffee. ;)

To Caitlin and Ellie. You two are my dream team and I am so glad I found you both! I can't imagine letting anyone else work on my books from here on out.

To the Minxes. You ladies rock! Seriously I found my tribe with all of you and I can't imagine trying to find my way through this book world without all of you. You put up with me every day and I am forever grateful.

To my Boss Babes. If someone would have told me three years ago that not only would I publish multiple books but that they would actually be read by non-family members I would have called them crazy. But yet here all of you are. You read my books, you chat with me on a daily basis, and I can't even believe it. I am so incredibly grateful for each and every one of you every day. You're the reason why I keep doing this. So, thank you!

And like always, to All Time Low. It's inevitable that every one of my book playlists will have one of your songs on it. Keep making your amazing music and I'll keep writing my books. No pressure or anything. ;)

ABOUT THE AUTHOR

 Born on a small southeastern island in Alaska and raised in southern Oregon, Alexandria Bishop is a PNW girl at heart. By day, she goes to battle with a tiny dictator aka her toddler and by night, she can be found typing ALL the words of her contemporary romance novels accompanied by a glass of wine or two ;)

When she's not in mommy or author mode, she can be found drinking copious amounts of cold brew coffee, bingeing her latest obsession on Netflix, or attending concerts of her favorite pop-punk bands.

She loves hearing from her readers and you can find her on social media here:

www.alexandriabishop.com
www.facebook.com/authoralexandriabishop
www.twitter.com/allieebishop
www.instagram.com/alexandria.bishop

88452092R00126

Made in the USA
Columbia, SC
02 February 2018